'I'm not interested in getting married again.

'My only concern is to take care of Jessica to the very best of my ability. Nothing else matters apart from that.'

'But surely you deserve a life of your own? You're a young man, Matt, and it's wrong to rule out the chance of finding personal happiness again!'

She couldn't hide her dismay and she heard him sigh. 'I don't have the time or inclination for another relationship. I have enough to do with work and taking care of Jess.'

'But if you met someone else then you could share Jessica's care. It would take some of the burden off you.'

'By off-loading it onto someone else, you mean? That wouldn't be fair. Jessica is my daughter and it is up to me to take care of her.'

He took a deep breath and she saw an expression of intense pain cross his face. 'It's the very least I can do, considering that I am responsible for what happened to her and her mother.'

Jennifer Taylor has been writing Mills & Boon®
romances for some time, but only recently discovered
Medical Romances™. She was so captivated by these
heart-warming stories that she immediately set out to
write them herself! As a former librarian who worked
in scientific and industrial research, Jennifer enjoys the
research involved with the writing of each book as well
as the chance it gives her to create a cast of wonderful
characters. When not writing or doing research for her
latest book, Jennifer's hobbies include reading, travel,
and walking her dog. She lives in the north-west of
England with her husband and children.

Recent titles by the same author:

THE ITALIAN DOCTOR
TOUCHED BY ANGELS
A VERY SPECIAL CHILD
A REAL FAMILY CHRISTMAS

AN ANGEL
IN HIS ARMS

BY
JENNIFER TAYLOR

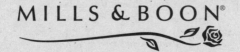

MILLS & BOON®

First published in Great Britain 2001
Harlequin Mills & Boon Limited,
Eton House, 18-24 Paradise Road, Richmond, Surrey TW9 1SR

© Jennifer Taylor 2001

ISBN 0 263 82674 0

Set in Times Roman 10½ on 11½ pt.
03-0701-54060

Printed and bound in Spain
by Litografía Rosés, S.A., Barcelona

CHAPTER ONE

'I AM delighted to tell you that we are offering you the job. Welcome to the air ambulance team, Miss Lennard. It's good to have you on board!'

Sharon Lennard gave a little gasp of delight. As soon as she had seen the advertisement for the post with the East Pennine Air Ambulance service, she had known that it was the job for her.

A fully qualified paramedic, she had given up her job in London the previous year to come home and nurse her father after he had suffered a stroke. He had died three months earlier, leaving her free to go back to work, but although she had enjoyed working in London, she had felt that she had needed a change. The post with the air ambulance service had seemed to fit the bill perfectly and she was thrilled that she would be working for them.

'Thank you so much!' she exclaimed, smiling at the people who had interviewed her. 'I can hardly believe that you've given *me* the job!'

'You were by far and away the best candidate, my dear,' Sir Humphrey Grey, Chief Executive of the air ambulance trust, assured her. 'We were all impressed by your references and the experience you've had. The key to running any successful service is the quality of its staff.'

He glanced at the younger man seated beside him. 'Dr Dempster joined us two years ago, and I hope he won't mind me saying that the figures have shown beyond any doubt that having a qualified doctor working with the team has proved invaluable. I am sure that your contribution will be just as vital. Don't you agree, Dr Dempster?'

'I very much hope so,' the younger man replied softly and in a tone that made Sharon frown because there seemed to be the faintest hint of doubt in it. She shot him a wary glance, wondering if she was letting her imagination run away with her.

Matthew Dempster hadn't said very much throughout her interview although she knew that he had been listening intently to everything she had said. In fact, she had been so aware of him that a couple of times she had found herself addressing her answers to him rather than to the person who had asked her the question. Why had it seemed so important that she should convince him of her worth?

Her eyes swept over him while she tried to work it out and she felt a little flurry dance along her nerves. Dr Dempster was almost sinfully good looking now that she had taken the time to really look at him! Dark haired, with thickly lashed green eyes and the most delectable dimple in his chin, he could easily have passed for a film star rather than a doctor. In fact, he would have been almost *too* perfect if it hadn't been for that slight crook in his nose…

'Miss Lennard?'

Sharon jumped guiltily when she realised that she had missed what Matthew Dempster had said to her. A little colour touched her cheeks as she hurriedly gathered her wits. The last thing she wanted was for the panel to start wondering if they'd given the job to the wrong person.

'I missed that, I'm afraid,' she explained as calmly as she could. She decided to brazen out her lapse and looked him straight in the eyes. 'I'm just so excited about being given this job, you understand.'

'Of course. However, I do hope that you manage to contain your excitement once you start working with us,' he replied smoothly and with so little emphasis that it somehow served to make the words seem all the more pointed. 'It's a job that demands a clear head at all times. We cannot afford to have someone on the team who allows herself to become…distracted.'

Sharon's hands clenched. It didn't help one jot to know that the rebuke had been justified because it wasn't that which had upset her. Had Matthew Dempster realised where her thoughts had been wandering just now? she wondered with a sinking heart.

The answer came back immediately as a resounding *yes*!

She forced herself to smile, determined that he wouldn't see how mortified she felt. 'Don't worry, Dr Dempster. I'm not prone to letting myself be distracted, especially not while I'm working. I assure you that I will have no difficulty whatsoever keeping my mind on the job.'

He inclined his head although he didn't say anything else. Consequently, Sharon had no idea whether she had managed to convince him. Fortunately, one of the other board members asked her a question then so she was able to focus on that, and for the rest of the time she was there Matthew Dempster remained silent.

She left the interview room some ten minutes later and heaved a sigh of relief. Was she glad that was over! Oh, the interview had been fine and the results even better. However, the fact that Matthew Dempster thought she had been daydreaming about him didn't sit well with her.

Maybe it was something that had happened in the past because he was certainly handsome enough to have set many a female heart fluttering. But looks weren't everything, as her father had been so fond of saying, and she would reserve judgement on Dr Dempster for the moment and make up her mind about him at some later date.

She was heading for the exit when it struck her that he might not afford her the same courtesy, and she groaned. Heaven only knew what kind of impression he had formed of her!

* * *

'And this is the staffroom. It's hardly five star luxury, as you can see, but it serves its purpose. Anyway, that's Bert Davies, the senior paramedic around here, stuffing himself with toast. And Andy Carruthers, your pilot, with his nose buried in a book as usual. And that unsavoury character in the corner is Mike Henderson, who claims to be one of the radio operators here at the base, although we're not convinced that he isn't just spinning us a line. Now, who have I missed out?'

It was her first day in the new job and Sharon was being shown around the air ambulance station. Beth Maguire, a paramedic on the opposite shift, had taken it upon herself to make the introductions.

Sharon smiled and said hello, mentally crossing her fingers that she would remember everyone's name. Frankly, her head seemed to have been in a spin ever since her interview because there had been so much to learn. In the past four weeks she had been on an intensive first-aid refresher course as well as doing courses in flight safety, navigation and communications. It felt as though her feet had hardly touched the ground and she hadn't even got up into the air yet!

'Oh, Matt, of course. How could I have forgotten him?' Beth laughed out loud at her oversight, mercifully missing Sharon's involuntary groan.

In the past month she had found her thoughts returning rather too frequently to Matthew Dempster and what had happened at her interview that day. She had to admit that she wasn't comfortable with the thought that he believed she had been daydreaming about him. The last thing she wanted was for him to think that she was the kind of woman who developed crushes on the men she worked with.

Still, with a bit of luck she wouldn't come into contact

with him all that often. With three teams all working a ten-hour shift system, it shouldn't be *that* difficult to avoid him.

'Does Dr Dempster work with your team?' she asked hopefully.

'I should be so lucky!' Beth declared. 'No, our delectable Dr Dempster will be working with you, and I'm positively green with envy. What I wouldn't give to spend quality time with that man… Aha, speak of the devil. We were just talking about you.'

Sharon swung round when Beth laughed. Matthew Dempster must have come up behind them without her noticing and she felt her heart ricochet around her chest when she saw him standing there. She tried her best not to stare but it was a losing battle from the outset.

Neon orange flight suits should have come way down the list of outfits that could be classed as *sexy*, but that depended on who was wearing them, she supposed. Matthew Dempster certainly looked good in his! His shoulders were broad enough to fill out the bulky fabric, whilst his waist and hips were trim enough not to look bulky at all. And as for his legs…

Sharon tore her appreciative gaze away from the long—very long!—legs that ended in a pair of sturdy boots and fixed them on a poster a little to the left of Dr Dempster's handsome head. The poster had a picture of a lost dog on it, with a number to call to claim a reward. She stared at it until she could have recited the details from memory because it seemed safer than being accused of letting herself get distracted again.

'I won't ask what you were saying,' Matthew said lightly yet Sharon heard the undercurrent in his voice and inwardly squirmed. Had he noticed her staring at him? she wondered, then quickly closed her mind to the answer because she didn't want to hear it.

'Wise man!' Beth retorted, glancing at her watch. 'Right,

looks like that's me out of here. Have fun, you two. Let's hope you don't end up paying for the blissfully quiet night we've had!'

She gave them a quick wave then hurried away. There was a lot of bustling about as the night shift left. Matthew waited until everything had quietened down before he turned to Sharon, and she felt her heart sink even further when she saw the cool look he gave her.

'I take it that Beth has given you the grand tour?'

'Yes. It…it was kind of her to show me round and introduce me to everyone,' she replied as calmly as she could in the circumstances. The thought that once again she might have blotted her copybook with this man before she'd even written anything on the first page didn't help soothe her first-day nerves.

'You need to get to know where everything is as fast as possible. Ditto the people you'll be working with. We work closely as a team and often in situations that could prove dangerous. We need to know that we can rely totally on one another.'

'I understand that,' she said quickly. 'And I'm used to working as part of a team. It's something that was drummed into us where I last worked.'

'Then you will understand why I won't tolerate any kind of disruptions to team harmony. That is why I prefer it if the staff working here keep their private lives and their working lives separate. I would take a very dim view of any member of staff becoming personally involved with a colleague.' His cool green eyes swept over her before coming back to her face. 'I hope you will bear that in mind.'

Sharon didn't know what to say. She was just too embarrassed by the fact that he had thought it necessary to issue the warning. Had she somehow given him the impression that she was trying to make a play for him?

Frankly, it was a situation she had never encountered

before. Normally, it was the men who came on to her, not the other way round. She wasn't vain but she was realistic enough to know that men found her attractive.

At five feet eight inches tall, with a naturally slim figure, she looked good in most outfits, and her current one, an orange flight suit that was a twin of the one Matthew was wearing, was no exception. The fact that the orange perfectly offset her russet gold hair and deep brown eyes was pure chance. She'd had no say in what she was wearing because it was the uniform they all wore. However, Matthew made her feel as though she had been deliberately flaunting herself for his benefit.

Sharon drew herself up to her full height and looked him straight in the eyes. 'I understand what you're saying, Dr Dempster. I assume this is something you tell all new staff and that you haven't singled me out for some reason?'

'Why should I single you out, Miss Lennard?' he countered smoothly. 'As a member of the team, you will be treated exactly the same as everyone else.'

He treated her to a last frosty smile then moved away. Sharon took a deep breath and counted to ten, but it didn't cool her bubbling temper. If she'd had to choose just one word to sum up Dr Matthew Dempster, it would have to be *arrogant*! Frankly, she would love to wipe the smile off his handsome face...

She sighed as she realised how foolish it was to think like that. It was hardly conducive to team harmony, was it? If Matthew Dempster had formed the wrong impression of her then that was his problem.

But was it? a small voice whispered. It could be her problem, too, if he chose to make life difficult for her, as he very well might.

She sighed again. Day one had really got off to a flying start!

* * *

The morning rushed past, although there were no emergency calls. Sharon was a little disappointed but she kept herself busy by going over all the things she had learned during her training. When Mike Henderson invited her into the control room to show her round, she eagerly accepted.

'Keeping in constant touch with base is absolutely vital,' he explained, tilting back his chair and putting his feet on the edge of the desk. He grinned at her, his boyishly attractive face lighting up in a way that immediately made her smile back. 'Think of me as the fount of all knowledge, Sharon, and you won't go far wrong.'

'Not that you're big-headed or anything,' she teased.

'Moi? I'm gutted that you could suggest such a thing!' He hung his head, trying his best to look hurt. 'I hope that doesn't mean you're one of those hard-hearted females who don't appreciate men?'

'Depends on the man,' she retorted, quickly suppressing all thoughts of Matthew Dempster. As far as she was concerned, the less she had to do with him the better, although it probably wasn't the best attitude in the circumstances. Still, teamwork involved *all* members of the team trying to get on so it was up to him to do his bit. She was willing to meet him halfway but that was as far as she intended to go.

'Anyway, why should I consider you to be the oracle? If you want my vote then you have to convince me.'

'Definitely not a pushover, are you?' Mike said with a laugh. 'OK, if you won't take my word for it then I suppose I shall have to outline my credentials, loath though I am to blow my own trumpet. When you're out on a shout…that's a call to the uninitiated…I'm the guy who not only checks you're on course but warns you of any hazards that your pilot might be unaware of.'

'What sort of hazards?' she asked curiously.

'Changes in the weather, possible problems that might

arise when you try to land, that kind of thing,' he explained. 'For example, we had a shout last week to a guy who had been injured in an RTA. Turned out that he and this other chap had been having a race when he'd overturned his car.

'The problem was that these two idiots weren't on their own but had their friends with them. I had to warn Andy not to land until the police gave me the all-clear because the two gangs were fighting. The police were afraid that they might turn on the helicopter if Andy had tried to set down.'

'Good heavens! Why would anyone want to attack the helicopter? Didn't they realise they could be putting their friend's life at risk if he couldn't be airlifted to hospital?'

'I don't suppose they cared one way or the other,' Mike said flatly. 'Anyway, you must have experienced that sort of situation yourself on occasion when you worked in London?'

'You're right. A couple of times things got a bit scary,' she admitted, then gave a rueful laugh. 'I thought I'd escape all that by working here!'

'No way. You need to be on your toes at all times—' Mike broke off and swung his feet to the floor when the alarm suddenly sounded. 'Action stations! Looks like it's time to earn your wings, kiddo.'

Sharon wasted no time as she raced out of the control room. Maybe if she hadn't been so keen to see what was happening she might have paused to check that there was no one coming along the corridor, but as it was she ran full tilt into Matthew.

'Careful!' He automatically put out a steadying hand as she rebounded off him, although she noticed that he let her go the moment she had regained her balance. Did he think that she had deliberately run into him, perhaps?

Her mouth thinned as she looked into his cold green eyes and saw her answer. She didn't know whether to laugh out loud or tear a strip off him because it was so ridiculous. In the end, she decided to treat it with the disdain it deserved.

'Sorry, I didn't see you. Do I take it that we're going out on a call?'

'Yes. A child injured in a riding accident. Possible spinal damage and needs immediate airlift to Leeds,' he explained, glancing at the incident report sheet he was holding.

'How long will it take us to get there?' Sharon asked as she followed him along the corridor.

'About fifteen minutes if the wind isn't against us.' He didn't pause as he headed for a door at the end of the corridor. Through the glass pane in its top, she could see the bright yellow helicopter sitting on its pad, and her mouth went dry when it hit her that she was about to be whisked up in the machine.

Matthew paused to look back when she faltered, and for a moment his expression softened so that she had a glimpse of a man who seemed a world removed from the aloof professional she had thought him to be.

'It will be fine, Sharon. You'll see.' He took a helmet off the peg marked with her name and offered it to her. 'Come on, let's get going. We've a patient to treat.'

She took a deep breath then exhaled sharply, and it felt as though her nerves had flowed away with it. She took the helmet from him and quickly opened the door. She felt him give her shoulder a squeeze as she passed, *thought* she heard him say, 'That's my girl!', but she could have been mistaken. The noise the helicopter was making was deafening, and she was hardly *his* girl, was she? Still, it all helped to put her at ease and that was the main thing.

She ran to the helicopter, bending low when she felt the upward draught from its rotors. Bert Davies was already on board and he gave her a helping hand inside. Sharon strapped herself in while Matthew climbed aboard and secured the door. A second later they were airborne. The town whizzed past beneath them with dizzying speed and she smiled in sudden delight. It felt really great!

She turned to the other two, wanting to know if they still felt the same rush of excitement each time they flew, and found her eyes caught by Matthew's. There was the strangest expression in them at that moment, something that looked almost like regret...

He turned to speak to Andy and she took a shuddering breath, deeply disturbed by what had happened. Why had he looked at her like that? Was it because he regretted that she had been given the job?

It seemed the most logical explanation yet she knew instinctively that it wasn't the only one and that the answer was far more complex. That worried her—a lot. She far preferred to know all the answers than be left with only questions.

'Can you see anything yet?'

Sharon leant forward as Matthew tapped Andy on the shoulder. They had been flying for roughly fifteen minutes and she guessed that they must be nearing the site of the accident. They had left the town behind some time before and were flying over open country now. To their left were the Pennines, the mountain range that formed the backbone of Britain. It was a particularly clear day and the view was breathtaking. However, they weren't there to admire the scenery and she was as eager as the others were to reach their destination.

'Not yet, but it shouldn't be long now,' Andy replied, his voice sounding distorted as it came through the headphones built into her helmet. 'Ah, if I'm not mistaken, there they are—roughly two miles at twelve o'clock.'

Sharon shifted further forward so that she could see where he was pointing. The air crew used a simple system for pinpointing locations. Using the dial of a clock as a guide, they would describe a visual sighting in terms of where the hour hand should be pointing. Thus two miles at twelve o'clock meant that they needed to land roughly two miles away and straight ahead.

It took only a few minutes to reach the landing site. Andy hovered overhead to check that there was nothing on the ground that might damage the helicopter's skids then gently set it down in the field. Matthew had the door open before the pilot had cut the engine.

'Bert, you bring the stretcher while Sharon comes with me,' he instructed.

Sharon jumped out of the helicopter and followed him at a run to where a group of people were gathered around a small figure lying on the ground. Matthew quickly introduced himself then knelt beside the child.

'What happened?' he asked as he started to examine the girl.

'Lucy was thrown from her pony. I don't know how it happened. Gypsy's usually so steady...' A woman, who was obviously the child's mother, gulped and the man standing beside her, whom Sharon assumed was the father, put a comforting arm around her.

'How did she land? Flat on her back or did she come down head first?' Matthew continued, gently running his hand along the child's spine. Sharon knew that he was testing for any obvious damage to the vertebrae but from the quick shake of his head realised that he hadn't found any.

She quickly checked the child's pulse and was unsurprised to find it rapid and thready. The little girl, who was about ten years old, was deeply unconscious and her face was waxen under the peak of her black riding hat. Sharon quickly ripped open a cannula and inserted it into the back of the child's hand, knowing that Matthew would want to get a line in as fast as possible to raise her fluid levels and counteract the effects of shock.

'She came straight over Gypsy's head and landed on her back, exactly as she is now. I haven't moved her because I was worried about damaging her spine,' the sobbing mother explained.

'Good. You did exactly the right thing,' he said encouragingly, rolling back the child's eyelids so he could check her pupils. The left one responded when he shone a light into it but the right was fixed and dilated. It was a sure sign that the little girl had suffered a head injury and Sharon knew that she would require urgent treatment.

'She is going to be all right, isn't she? I mean, it was only a bit of tumble. I expect she's just winded.'

Matthew gestured to Bert to bring over the stretcher before he answered the father's question. Sharon concentrated on setting up the drip, handing the bag of fluid to one of the bystanders to hold while she helped the other paramedic fit a cervical collar around the child's neck. The routine was so familiar that she didn't wait for instructions but just got on with the job. The sooner they got Lucy to hospital the greater her chances of recovery would be.

'I'm afraid I can't give you any definite answers at this stage,' Matthew said quietly, carefully palpating the child's abdomen while he checked for signs of internal damage. Once again he gave a slight negative shake of his head when Sharon glanced at him, and she breathed a little sigh of relief.

'Your daughter has suffered a serious head injury and we need to get her to hospital straight away so she can be treated. They'll also check to see if there are any other injuries,' he explained in the same calm tone, while Bert lined up the stretcher next to the child. 'I can't find any indication of internal injuries but she will need to be X-rayed to confirm that.'

'But it can't be that bad,' the man persisted. 'I fell off my horse umpteen times when I was a lad, but apart from a few bruises I never really hurt myself.'

'Maybe not, but I'm afraid Lucy hasn't been so lucky,' Matthew replied, a shade curtly this time. Sharon looked at him curiously but it was impossible to tell what was wrong and it certainly wasn't the time to start asking.

The man fell silent, obviously deciding that it was better not to say anything else. However, she couldn't help thinking that Matthew had been a bit hard on him. It was normal for parents to enter a state of denial after a child had been injured. Some found it impossible to accept that the situation was potentially life-threatening. She was rather surprised that Matthew seemed not to have taken that into account, but there was no time to dwell on it when their first priority was to get the girl to hospital.

The three of them carefully shifted the limp little body onto the stretcher and Bert covered her with a blanket. Sharon secured the safety straps then retrieved the bag of intravenous fluid and glanced at Matthew. 'Ready.'

'Right, let's go.' He took one end of the stretcher and Bert took the other as they ran to the helicopter. The child's parents hurried after them and he spoke briefly to them once they had loaded the child on board.

'We're taking Lucy straight to Leeds. I'm sorry, but we haven't room to take you as well.'

'Don't worry about us. Just get her there as fast as you can.' The child's mother laid a beseeching hand on his arm. 'Take care of her for me, Doctor, won't you? She's very precious.'

'I shall.' Matthew's expression softened as he squeezed the woman's hand. Sharon was shocked to see a look of real pain cross his face before he turned and climbed on board. He reverted to normal immediately and began rattling out instructions, but she was puzzled by what she had witnessed. As a doctor he would be bound to feel concerned for a patient, yet there had been something far more personal to it than that.

It was all very strange but she had no time to think about it as the helicopter prepared to take off. They lifted off smoothly and Andy turned the machine in a graceful arc so that they could head to Leeds. She could see the child's anxious parents staring up at them and her heart ached for what they must have been going through. It must be dreadful to watch your child being whisked away and not be able to go with her. Without stopping to think, she voiced the thought out loud.

'If they'd had the sense not to let the poor kid ride in the first place then this would never have happened,' Matthew said harshly. 'I find it incredible that parents allow their children to take unnecessary risks.'

'You can't wrap children up in cotton wool,' Sharon countered in surprise. 'You have to let them try things even if they do hold a certain degree of risk.'

'I wonder if Lucy's parents are going to feel it was worth the risk if she doesn't pull through?' he snapped back. 'There are enough dangers in this life without deliberately taking chances.'

She was so amazed by his attitude that she opened her mouth to argue the point, only just then Bert nudged her sharply in the ribs. She glanced at him but he shook his head. It was obvious that he was warning her against saying anything more, but why? Was this another of Dr Dempster's fiercely held views, that *underlings* shouldn't argue with him? So much for teamwork!

Sharon stayed silent for the rest of the journey. Matthew handed Lucy over to the staff waiting to receive her and they were heading back to base a few minutes later. Bert and Andy kept up a desultory conversation on the flight but neither she nor Matthew joined in. Frankly, Sharon didn't trust herself not to say something about his overbearing attitude so deemed it wiser to stay silent, and he certainly didn't make any attempt to draw her out. Was she in the doghouse again for daring to air her views? Probably!

It was a little after one when they landed. Matthew had a brief word with Andy then climbed out of the helicopter and went straight inside but Bert hung back to wait for her. Sharon smiled ruefully at the middle-aged paramedic.

'I'm glad you're talking to me. Ever had the feeling that you've got off to a bad start?'

Bert laughed, although she couldn't help noticing that he looked a shade uncomfortable. 'Rubbish. You're not going to have any trouble doing this job, Sharon. You handled today's incident like a real pro.'

'Thanks.' She sighed as she stared at Matthew's retreating back. 'I don't suppose you'd like to repeat that for our revered leader's benefit? I seem to have a positive knack for putting my foot in it when he's around.'

'You mean what happened earlier?' Bert sighed when she nodded. 'I was hoping you'd take the hint and not say anything else.'

'Why? Is it really such a crime to have an opinion that differs to that of the great Dr Dempster's?' she demanded hotly. 'He's already told me that he doesn't like his staff getting too friendly. I think you'd better tell me what other rules I shouldn't break.'

'I don't know about rules. I expect Matt is just anxious to avoid the kind of situation we had a few months back,' Bert explained. 'Your predecessor, Amanda, was going out with one of the paramedics off B shift. Unfortunately, when they split up things got rather difficult. You could have cut the atmosphere with a knife whenever they met up.

'In the end Matt gave them both an ultimatum—they either kept their private lives away from work or they found other jobs. Amanda resigned soon afterwards. It was her choice, mind. Matt certainly didn't push her into it. He'd made his position clear and that would have been the end of it. Still, everyone was relieved when she went because there'd been a few other problems with her as well.'

'I see,' Sharon said softly. It certainly helped to explain why Matt had seen fit to issue that warning to her. A situation like that must have been highly detrimental to the smooth running of the service.

'Anyhow, the reason I was nudging you was because I realised that you had no idea about Matt's circumstances,' Bert continued. 'I didn't want you saying the wrong thing.'

'What circumstances?' she asked automatically, only half listening. Although she sympathised with Matthew, the thought that he was comparing her to the other woman still irked her. She was too much of a professional to let her private life interfere with her work…

She caught the tail end of what Bert had said and it drove everything else out of her head. 'Say that again,' she exclaimed.

'That Matt has a daughter who's disabled as the result of an accident,' he repeated obligingly. 'Poor kid was with her mother when a van mounted the pavement and ran them down. Jessica survived but she's been in a wheelchair ever since. As for his wife…well, there was nothing anyone could do for her.

'The worst thing was that Matt was on duty when they were both taken to the hospital. God knows what he must have gone through that day—it doesn't bear thinking about. But he's entitled to take a hard line occasionally, in my opinion. He's certainly paid his dues.'

Bert gave her a resigned smile then headed inside. Andy said something to her in passing but Sharon had no idea what it was. Her mind seemed to have frozen on an image of Matthew's face when he had held Lucy's mother's hand.

No wonder he had looked so anguished! He must have

been thinking about what had happened to his own daughter. It also explained why he had been so dogmatic about children not being allowed to take risks. It made her own views seem so crassly insensitive all of a sudden that she was stricken with remorse. She owed him an apology and there was no way that she would shirk it.

She hurried inside and went straight to the office. She had actually raised her hand to knock on the door when it struck her that she might be committing another error. Why should Matthew want to hear how sorry she was? It certainly wouldn't make up in any way for what had happened to him, and her heart ached at the thought.

Her hand fell to her side. Matthew Dempster wasn't the least bit interested in her or her apologies.

CHAPTER TWO

THEY had another call later that afternoon. A premature baby needed airlifting to a specialist neo-natal unit on Merseyside. Matthew called everyone into the office to finalise the arrangements.

'The baby will be transported in a specially heated and ventilated incubator,' he explained for Sharon's benefit. 'The helicopter is equipped with a power point for such eventualities, although the incubator has its own battery-operated generator as a back up.'

'Always best to avoid any unnecessary risks,' she replied without thinking. She felt her cheeks warm when he treated her to a chilly smile. Did Matthew think that had been a dig at him for what he had said earlier? she wondered with a sinking heart.

'It certainly is. We aren't in the business of taking risks with people's lives, which is why planning and preparation are so important.'

He looked up when Andy came into the room and she breathed a sigh of relief at having been let off so lightly. She really must be more careful about what she said, although it was going to be a strain, having to watch every word. However, it would be worth it if it meant that she wouldn't unwittingly remind Matthew of his past unhappiness.

It was a surprise to realise how much she wanted to avoid doing that. Matthew had hardly gone out of his way to avoid hurting *her* feelings but that didn't seem to matter. The thought of what he must have gone through when his wife had died made her heart ache in the strangest way.

'I've been on to air-traffic control and they've promised to clear a flight path for us,' Andy briskly informed them. He unrolled the chart he was carrying and laid it on the desk, pointing to an area outlined in red. 'There's no problem at that end so picking up the child is going to be our biggest headache. There are no landing facilities at the hospital so the police are looking for an alternative site for us to set down.'

'I see.' Matthew turned to Sharon once more. 'This is a problem we encounter all too often. Finding a suitable landing area for the helicopter can prove extremely difficult at times. Unfortunately, there are lots of hospitals within our catchment area which don't have helipads so it isn't only when we are called to the site of an accident that we experience problems.'

'So what will happen today?' she queried. 'Will the police find a field or somewhere like that for us to land?'

'Probably. They're searching the area now. Once they've found a suitable site we can arrange for an ambulance from the hospital to transport the baby over there to meet us.' He shrugged. 'It all takes a bit of extra time but we need to have everything worked out in advance to avoid any mishaps.'

'What kind of mishaps?' she asked immediately, wanting to learn all she could about her new job. The more she knew then the easier it would be for her to become a valuable member of the team, she reasoned.

'Things like overhead power cables have to be taken into account for starters. Andy can't land if there are cables strung all across the place. Then we have to know that the ground is suitable for landing and that the police can keep the area clear. The last thing we need is a crowd of excited spectators getting in the way when we're trying to land,' he added dryly.

Sharon laughed at the rueful note in his voice. 'Sounds as though that may have happened a time or two.'

He chuckled. 'More times than any of us care to count, I'm afraid. There's just *something* about a helicopter that attracts attention.'

'No wonder!' she retorted. 'It may be commonplace to you lot, but having a helicopter land in the middle of your local playing field isn't an everyday occurrence for most people, me included!'

Andy laughed. 'Does anyone else get the impression that our Sharon is overwhelmed by the glamour of this job?'

'I am! And I make no apologies for it. Why do you think I applied for it in the first place?'

It had been meant as a joke and everyone laughed—everyone apart from Matthew, that was. 'You'll soon find that there is nothing very glamorous about what we do. We're in this business to save lives and the fact that we use a helicopter to do so is incidental. Anyone who has been seduced by the image won't last long, I'm afraid.'

Sharon's cheeks burned at the undeserved reprimand. 'I know that. I was only joking as it happens. I can assure you that I have enough experience of working with injured people to know that there's nothing at all glamorous about it.'

There was a small uncomfortable silence after she had finished. It made her wonder if she had been a bit too quick to respond. However, she had meant every word and there was no way that she intended to back down.

Bert cleared his throat. 'From what I've seen today, Sharon, you have nothing to prove. You know what you're doing, that's for sure.'

'Thanks.' She gave him a grateful smile but she was very aware that Matthew didn't say anything to endorse the paramedic's view. Fortunately, the telephone rang at that point.

Matthew quickly picked up the receiver and spoke briefly to the caller.

'That was the police to say that they've found a suitable landing site for us,' he told them, jotting down a series of numbers on the pad. He tore off the sheet and handed it to Andy. 'These are the co-ordinates if you want to have a word with Mike.'

The pilot hurried from the room as he turned to her and Bert. 'There's no point you both coming along. I suggest that you stay here, Bert, and finish writing up the report of this morning's incident while Sharon comes with me.'

She was a little surprised that he had decided she should accompany him but she didn't question the decision. Not only did she want to go along, she also knew that it would be a mistake. Bert seemed quite happy to be left behind anyway, so she was confident that she wasn't creating any waves.

Matthew led the way to the helicopter and climbed on board, holding out a hand to help her. Sharon quickly suppressed a shiver as she felt the coolness of his fingers closing around hers. For some reason the old saying about cold hands and warm heart sprang to mind but that hardly seemed appropriate. Maybe Matthew had possessed a warm heart once upon a time but she guessed that things had changed greatly for him since his wife had died.

She strapped herself in, studying him covertly as he leant forward to speak to Andy. It was hard to imagine how he might have behaved before that terrible accident. She simply didn't know him well enough to fill in the gaps. Yet deep down she suspected that the coolly detached face he presented to the world was simply a mask to hide his real feelings.

'We should be there in roughly twenty minutes.'

Matthew's voice coming through her headphones made

her jump and she raised startled eyes to his face. 'Oh… right. Where have the police found for us to land, then?'

'A school playing field on the outskirts of the town. Evidently, the kids are using it at the moment for an inter-school league football match but the police have promised to clear the area before we get there.' He gave her a totally unexpected smile. 'Looks as though we're going to have a big audience though, Sharon, so this could be your fifteen minutes of fame!'

She was so startled by his teasing that it took her a second to respond. She uttered a delighted laugh, marvelling at how her heart had instantly lifted because he had seen fit to unbend a little. 'I can hardly wait. I only wish I'd thought to wear something suitably glamorous for the occasion!'

Andy gave a snort of laughter. 'Maybe we should think of putting in a request for gold lamé flight suits, eh, Matt? It does seem a shame to disappoint our fans.'

Matthew laughed. 'I can just imagine what we would look like, too!' His gaze swept over Sharon and she felt her blood heat when his eyes came back to her face. 'I think Sharon would put the rest of us in the shade anyway, so it hardly seems worth it. With her around I doubt anyone will be looking at us.'

She didn't know what to say because the compliment had been so unexpected. Fortunately, he didn't seem to expect her to say anything so she let the subject drop. However, that didn't mean she could forget about it. One tiny corner of her brain had already logged it for future reference…

She sighed. What a pathetic creature she was to start making something out of nothing! Matt had been teasing her and even though it had been a surprise—or rather, a *shock*—she mustn't read too much into it. One small compliment certainly didn't make a relationship!

They touched down some twenty minutes later. Sharon could see quite a crowd gathered around the perimeter of the playing field and understood why Matt preferred to know that the police would be around to contain any overly enthusiastic spectators.

He opened the helicopter's door and jumped down as the ambulance made its way over the grass to meet them. Sharon climbed out as well, taking off her helmet and quickly shaking back her hair. Normally, she would have confined the shoulder-length russet waves into a chignon for work but she had discovered during training that her helmet fitted better if she left her hair loose. She had also been advised to avoid any sort of slides or pins as they could prove hazardous in the event of an emergency landing. An innocent-looking hair-slide could cause quite severe damage if it became embedded in the skull.

Out of the corner of her eyes she saw a bright flash and glanced round to see a photographer pointing his camera their way. Seeing he had her attention, he came hurrying over, neatly sidestepping the policeman who tried to stop him.

'Geoff Goodison from the local *Weekly News*. How long have you been working with the air ambulance service?'

'I only started today,' she answered automatically, her attention on what was happening as the ambulance drew up. She took a step towards it then stopped when the reporter laid a detaining hand on her arm.

'Can you tell me your name? Our readers love a good human interest story,' he demanded.

'Sharon Lennard.' She smiled apologetically. 'Sorry, I've got to go.'

He let her go, moving out of the way as the policeman

came over to ask him to leave. Sharon hurried over to the ambulance as it came to a halt. Matt looked round when she joined him and she couldn't help noticing the forbidding expression on his face.

'Try to keep your mind on the job, will you, Sharon? If and when we need to publicise the work we do, I shall let you know, but at the moment we have a very sick baby to think about.'

She was so astounded by the reprimand that she couldn't think of anything to say in her own defence. He had made it sound as though she had been deliberately *courting* the attentions of the photographer, rather than it having been the other way round.

Her lips snapped together because it wasn't the time or the place to argue the point. But that didn't mean she intended to let him get away with it. Life was going to be very difficult if every time she turned round Matt accused her of doing something wrong.

The ambulance crew carefully unloaded the incubator and transferred it to the waiting helicopter. The baby's father had come along to see her off and he drew Sharon aside.

'She will be all right, won't she? Promise me that you'll take care of her.' His eyes filled with tears. 'The doctors don't know if her mother is going to make it, you see. I don't think I could bear to lose the baby as well.'

Sharon patted his arm, feeling her own eyes tear up at what he must be going through. 'We'll take good care of her, I promise you.'

'Thanks.' He dredged up a smile as he looked at the incubator. 'Her name's Chloe…Chloe Richardson. It took us ages to decide what to call her.'

'It's a beautiful name,' she said quietly. She looked round when Matt called out to let her know they were ready to leave. 'We have to go now. Try not to worry. We'll look after Chloe.'

She quickly climbed on board and Matt secured the doors. The incubator had been anchored to the fuselage by means of metal clamps to stop it moving around during the flight. Sharon strapped herself in then quickly checked the baby's status, using the monitoring equipment that was attached to the state-of-the-art incubator. She ran an experienced eye over the printout and was relieved to see that Chloe's condition didn't appear to be deteriorating.

'How is she?' Matt asked.

'She seems to be holding her own,' Sharon told him, passing him the monitor readings.

He skimmed through the figures then sighed as he looked at the tiny child. 'It's hard to believe that any child so small can survive, yet they achieve wonderful results with babies weighing even less than she does.'

'Do you think she'll make it?' Sharon asked, unaware of the wistful note that had crept into her voice. She glanced at the notes that had accompanied the baby. 'Respiratory distress syndrome, jaundice, hypoglycaemia—that's a lot of problems for something so tiny.'

'Babies are surprisingly tough. Some overcome the most incredible odds,' Matt said quietly. 'The fact that she's got this far is a good sign. We'll just have to focus on the thought that she'll soon be receiving the very best care.'

He smiled at her and Sharon smiled back, feeling comforted by what he'd said. Obviously the baby was very sick but the fact that she would soon be in a specialist unit would greatly increase her chances of survival, as Matt had pointed out.

The flight to Merseyside was uneventful. Andy kept in close radio contact with the air-traffic controllers at both Manchester and Liverpool airports and, as promised, they cleared a path for them. Sharon found herself wondering if they had delayed any of the planes leaving the airports, and asked Andy.

'We fly at a much lower altitude than the commercial aircraft,' he explained, 'so we won't have caused any problems. It's a good job, too, otherwise there would have been a lot of unhappy people this afternoon.'

'I'm sure people would have understood if they had been delayed,' she protested. 'Nobody would have minded being held up if they'd known that we were taking a sick baby to hospital.'

Matt laughed shortly. 'Do you really think that would make any difference? In my experience people are so bound up in their own lives that they don't spare much thought for anyone else.'

It was such a stark view, all the more so coming on top of the way he had tried to reassure her about Chloe's chances of survival. 'I don't agree,' she declared. 'All right, so there are always some folk who are so self-centred that they couldn't care less about other people, but the majority do care and want to help.'

'Your faith in mankind is touching, Sharon. I only hope that you aren't brought down to earth with a bump. Take it from me that most people couldn't give a damn about anyone else so long as they aren't inconvenienced.'

She shivered when she heard the harsh edge in his voice. She couldn't help wondering what had caused him to have such a bleak outlook on life. Was it a legacy from his wife's death, perhaps?

It seemed the most likely explanation and once again she felt her heart ache for him. It would be difficult to get over such a loss and obviously Matt was still suffering. His whole life must have changed on the day of the accident, as must his daughter's. Not only had the child lost her mother she had been left crippled as well.

If there had been anything she could have done to make

up for what had happened, she would have done it willingly. However, she guessed that Matt would rebuff her offers of help.

He didn't know her well enough yet to want to share his problems with her. She also suspected that he had no intention of getting to know her better in the future. Matt meant to keep her in the compartment labelled 'colleague'. How she knew that was a mystery, as was the reason why the thought hurt so much. It was all very unsettling. As first days went this was turning into something of a surprise for any number of reasons.

'Right, so who's for a drink, then?'

There were just five minutes to go before the end of their shift when Mike came into the staffroom. 'Seeing as it's Sharon's first day, we can't let the occasion pass unnoticed. How about a drink to celebrate her earning her wings, guys?'

'Sounds good to me,' Andy agreed immediately. 'Although, to be frank, she handled everything like such a pro that I'd almost forgotten it was her first day.'

Sharon laughed. 'Oh, flattery like that will get you *anywhere*, Mr Carruthers! In fact, I'll even buy you that drink.'

'Hey, don't forget it was my idea,' Mike chimed in. 'If there's free drinks going begging then I'd hate to miss out.'

'I can't imagine you missing out on *anything*, Mike Henderson!' she retorted, making everyone laugh. 'Anyway, I shall happily extend the offer of a free drink to everyone.'

'Attagirl! I knew you were going to be a welcome addition to this team.' Mike gave her a friendly hug then looked round when the door opened. 'Hey, Matt, you timed that just right. Sharon is buying us all a drink to celebrate her first day in the job.'

Sharon felt her face suffuse with colour when she saw

Matt standing in the doorway. She could imagine how it must have looked to him when he'd walked in and seen her standing there with Mike's arm around her. She couldn't help thinking back to what Bert had told her about her predecessor.

She quickly set some distance between herself and the young radio operator but she couldn't help noticing the expression of annoyance that crossed Matt's face before his customary mask slid into place.

'Thanks, but I'm afraid I have to get straight home,' he said coolly. 'I just thought you'd all like to know that the child we picked up this morning from that riding accident has regained consciousness. The CAT scan showed some minor swelling to her brain but the consultant is fairly confident that she hasn't suffered any long-term damage.'

'That's great!' Sharon declared, forgetting her own unease at the cheering news. 'Her parents must be so relieved.'

'I expect so.' He didn't say anything more before he left the room. Sharon wasn't sure what prompted her to go after him but she found herself following him out into the corridor. He stopped and looked back, his dark brows arching questioningly when he saw her.

'Yes?'

Did he really need to speak to her in that deliberately offhand manner? Sharon wondered, irritated by his attitude. Her spine stiffened, although she wasn't sure why it should hurt so much to have him treat her that way. Maybe Matt always behaved like this with people he didn't know very well, but it was hardly conducive to team harmony.

'Exactly what have you got against me, Matt? And before you start claiming that you've treated me like one of the team I have to tell you that it doesn't feel like that from where I'm standing.'

'Then all I can do is apologise,' he said flatly. 'If I've given you that impression then obviously I am at fault.'

She was so surprised by the apology that she found herself searching for an excuse for him. 'I imagine it's difficult to introduce a new member into the team.'

'It is, but that isn't the point. Obviously, I've handled things badly today and you are quite within your rights to draw my attention to it. The last thing I want is to cause any friction within the team. All I can do is repeat my apology and assure you that I shall be more careful in future.'

He treated her to a brief nod then went into his office. Sharon stayed where she was, wondering why she felt so dissatisfied. Matt had apologised and there was no doubt that he had been sincere, so what was troubling her now?

She sighed when she realised it was the fact that he had been so cold with her. Having felt the difference it had made when he had teased her on the way to pick up that prem baby, she couldn't help wishing for a bit more warmth from him.

'What are you doing out here? Don't tell me you were trying to skip out without buying us that drink?'

Mike suddenly appeared and Sharon made a determined effort to shake off the moment of introspection. Matt had apologised and everything was going to be rosy from now on.

'Would I do that?' she declared, going back into the staffroom to collect her bag. 'I promised you guys a drink and I never renege on a promise!'

'Glad to hear it.' Andy winked at the others. 'Although you must be a rare woman indeed if you keep *every* promise you make.'

Sharon laughed, unable to take offence at the teasing. 'Sounds to me like you've been mixing with the wrong type of women.'

'Tell me about it!' the pilot declared, rolling his eyes. 'You're speaking to the guy who's just notched up his third divorce.'

'And looking for victim number four, I shouldn't wonder,' Mike put in. He looped an arm around Sharon's shoulders and steered her towards the door. 'Stay well clear of our dashing captain is my advice. Stick to someone who keeps his feet firmly on the ground at all times.'

She grinned as she whisked out of his hold. 'I think I'm old enough not to need any advice about my love life, thank you, Uncle Mike!'

'That's what they all say but you can't put an old head on young shoulders,' he replied in the quavery voice of an octogenarian.

Everyone laughed as they headed out of the building. There was a pub next door and they piled into the bar. The conversation was very light-hearted and Sharon enjoyed herself. It was a good opportunity to get to know everyone better. However, as she made her way home an hour or so later she couldn't help thinking back to her claim that she didn't need any advice on her love life.

Maybe she didn't but that was because it was non-existent and had been for over a year. She'd been going out with one of the junior doctors from the hospital in London where she had worked, but the relationship had petered out when she had moved home to look after her father.

Sharon had been upset at first because she'd been fond of Steve Black and had thought that he'd felt the same way about her. However, he had grown impatient when she had been unable to leave her father to travel down to London to see him, and the only time he had visited her had been a disaster. Steve had wanted all her attention and had been unwilling to accept that she couldn't just go out and leave her father alone for hours on end.

Sharon had soon got over her disappointment, mainly because she had been too busy in the past year to worry about her social life. Still, there would be time for all that later. For now she had a great new job to concentrate on and a bunch of people she liked to work with. Frankly, the future had never seemed rosier!

Unbidden, an image of Matthew Dempster sprang to mind and she couldn't prevent the small sigh that escaped her. If only Matt's future were half as rosy as hers.

CHAPTER THREE

BY THE end of her first week, Sharon was confident that she had made the right decision by accepting the post with the air ambulance service. She loved the work and liked the people she worked with. Matt had been true to his word and their initial difficulties seemed to have been ironed out, although she still wished that he would treat her with a bit more warmth. The weather had continued to be fine so once she had finished all the jobs that needed doing in the bungalow where she and her father had moved to after his stroke, she decided to go into town. A bit of retail therapy was called for, to celebrate her first successful week back at work.

She changed into cream linen trousers and an olive-green silk shirt then drove into town. It was very busy because it was market day on Saturday, but that didn't worry her. Shopping had been a headache while she'd been caring for her father because she'd always been in a rush to get home. However, she had all the time in the world that day and made the most of it as she wandered around the stalls, although she couldn't help noticing that people seemed to be staring at her. It wasn't until she stopped at a bric-à-brac stall to buy a small porcelain vase which had caught her eye that she discovered why.

'You're Sharon Lennard, aren't you?' the stallholder said, deftly wrapping the vase in newspaper. 'You work for the air ambulance service.'

Sharon was completely taken aback. 'Yes, but how did you know that?'

'Oh, I've seen your picture, love.' The man delved under

the trestle table that served as a counter and handed her a newspaper. 'It's a lovely photo, too.'

Sharon gasped when she saw her picture splashed across the front page of the local weekly rag. It was the photo that had been taken the day they had airlifted the prem baby and she had forgotten all about it. It was a nice enough picture but the accompanying headline, NEW ANGEL EARNS HER WINGS, made her wince. She could imagine the ribbing she was going to get from the rest of the team when they saw it!

'Thanks. I hadn't seen it,' she explained, handing it back. She offered the stallholder the money for the vase but he shook his head.

'It's on me, love. My boy was in an accident last year and it was your lot who saved his life. The doctors at the hospital said that he wouldn't have stood a chance if the air ambulance hadn't got him there so quickly. People like you are worth your weight in gold, in my opinion.'

'Why, thank you. That's really kind of you.' Sharon was deeply touched by the gesture. She said goodbye and carried on with her shopping, thinking how wonderful it was to be part of an organisation that made such a difference to people's lives…

'Oof!' She gasped in surprise when something cannoned into the back of her, causing her to drop the vase, which promptly smashed as it hit the cobbles. She turned to remonstrate with whoever was responsible and was surprised to find that it was a little girl in a wheelchair who had run into her.

'I'm sorry. I didn't mean to do that.' The child's lower lip wobbled ominously as she stared at the broken vase. 'I didn't know there was a slope, you see, and I couldn't stop my chair.'

'It's all right,' Sharon quickly assured her, bending down. 'It was just an accident so don't cry.' She glanced along the busy street and frowned. 'Isn't there anyone with you?'

'My daddy's in that shop over there.' The little girl, who looked to be about eight years old, pointed to a butcher's shop further up the street. 'He couldn't get my chair up the steps so he had to leave me outside.'

'Oh, I see.' Sharon frowned when she saw the steep steps leading into the shop. Like most able-bodied people, she had rarely given any thought to the difficulties encountered by the disabled in the course of their daily lives. However, it struck her what a problem it must be, especially for parents caring for a disabled child. Things like having to leave them outside because they couldn't get a wheelchair into a shop must be a constant worry for them.

The thought had barely crossed her mind when a man came rushing out of the shop and began frantically scouring the street. Sharon gasped as she realised that it was Matthew Dempster. However, before she'd had time to really absorb that fact, he spotted them and came hurrying over.

'What the hell do you think you're doing?' he demanded, glaring at her. 'Haven't you more sense than to take a child away like that?'

She was so unprepared for the accusation that she could only stare at him in amazement. He muttered something uncomplimentary when she didn't answer then crouched down beside the wheelchair.

'Are you all right, sweetheart?'

'I'm fine, Daddy.' The little girl's lip began to wobble once more. 'Don't be cross with the lady because it wasn't her fault. I wanted to see the rabbits, you see, but my chair wouldn't stop and I bumped into her and made her drop her vase!'

Tears began to pour down her cheeks and Matt sighed as he put his arms around her. 'I told you I would take you to see the rabbits when we had finished our shopping. It was a very silly thing to do, Jess, and I want you to promise that you won't do it again. You mustn't go away when I've told you to wait for me.'

He rose to his feet as the little girl nodded. 'It seems that I owe you an apology, Sharon. I didn't mean to bite your head off like that, but I got the fright of my life when I looked out of the window and realised that Jessica had disappeared.'

There was no doubt that he was telling the truth and Sharon's tender heart ached as she realised what a scare he'd had. Without stopping to think, she laid a comforting hand on his arm. 'It's all right, Matt. I understand. I expect I would have done the same in your place.'

'Maybe, but I was too quick to jump in when I should have waited to hear what had really happened.' He gave her a rueful smile then bent to pick up the broken vase, effectively dislodging her hand. 'I'm sorry about this. If you'll tell me how much it cost I shall be happy to pay for a replacement.'

He took his wallet out of his pocket but she shook her head. Maybe it was silly to feel hurt because he had deliberately rebuffed her but she couldn't help it.

'Don't worry about it,' she assured him in a tight little voice. 'It wasn't expensive and, anyway, the stallholder wouldn't let me pay for it.'

His brows rose. 'Why ever not?'

She could have bitten off her tongue for saying that. Did she really want to have to explain about that photograph? Maybe she was being overly sensitive but she didn't want to give him another excuse to take her to task.

'Oh, maybe he was feeling generous. I don't know. Anyway, I mustn't keep you from your shopping.'

She bent down and smiled at the child, thinking how little she resembled her father. Jessica's hair was a very

pale blonde and her eyes blue. Sharon couldn't help wondering if the child took after her mother and if that made
the situation more or less difficult for Matt.

Was it a comfort to be reminded of his dead wife each
time he looked at his daughter, or did it make his loss all
the harder to bear? She had no idea, neither did she think
he would welcome her asking him such a personal question.

'It was lovely to meet you, Jessica. Just make sure that
you don't go giving your daddy any more frights like that.
You don't want his hair turning grey, do you?'

Jessica giggled. 'Daddy keeps saying that I'll make his
hair go grey but it hasn't happened yet!'

Sharon laughed as she shot an assessing look upwards.
'Oh, I think I can see the odd silver strand or two.'

'No wonder when this little madam pulls stunts like
that!'

Matt's face broke into a smile as he looked at his daughter. Sharon felt her breath catch when she saw how it had
changed him. He looked so different when he smiled like
that, so much more approachable. It was like being given
a glimpse of the person he must have been before tragedy
had touched his life.

The thought was more poignant than it should have been.
It was a relief when Jessica suddenly claimed their atten-
tion. 'Can we go and look at the rabbits now, Daddy?
Please!'

'I need to finish the shopping first, poppet.' He suddenly
groaned. 'Drat! I've left the meat on the butcher's counter.
I'll have to go back and get it. Ever had the feeling that
it's going to be one of those days when you take two steps
forward and three back?'

Sharon laughed at the rueful note in his voice. 'Frequently!' She glanced at the shop, and the steps leading up
to it, and knew she couldn't walk away without offering
to help.

'Look, why don't I take Jessica to see the rabbits while you go back for your meat? In fact, if you still have other shopping to do, why don't you go and get it? It will save you having to leave her outside again.'

'Oh, I don't think so—' he began, but didn't get a chance to finish when Jessica clapped her hands in delight.

'Yes! Oh, say that I can go, Daddy…please! I'm dying to see the rabbits and Sharon can take me.'

Matt sighed as he looked at his eight-year-old daughter's pleading face. 'I'm sure Sharon has things of her own to do, Jess. It isn't fair to bother her.'

'It's no trouble,' Sharon quickly assured him when she saw the little girl's face fall. She gave him a reassuring smile, sensing that his reluctance to accept her help stemmed more from parental concern than anything else. 'I'll take really good care of Jessica, I promise.'

He seemed to make up his mind all at once. 'All right, then, if you're sure. It's so busy today that it's a nightmare trying to negotiate this crowd with a wheelchair.' He pointed to the pet stall. 'That's where I promised to take Jess. I'll meet you over there in…what? Fifteen minutes' time?'

'Fine,' Sharon agreed, taking hold of the handles of the chair. She wheeled the little girl towards the stall, knowing without having to look that Matt was watching them. It was very strange the way the skin on the back of her neck prickled as his eyes rested on her. She knew to the second when he turned away and breathed a sigh not of relief but of bewilderment. How could she have *felt* him looking at her?

Fortunately, she had no time to dwell on it. The sheer physical effort of wheeling Jessica over the bumpy cobblestones demanded all her concentration. Jessica giggled and grabbed hold of the chair arms when it bounced over a particularly large bump.

'This is fun! Daddy never does this.'

Out of the mouths of babes, Sharon thought wryly. She took even more care, trying to avoid the worst of the ruts, but she was out of breath by the time they reached the pet stall even if Jessica looked as though she'd been having the time of her life. The difficulties of caring for a disabled child were far more varied than she had imagined!

Jessica was mesmerised by the rabbits in their straw-filled hutches. She put her face against the wire mesh and stared at them in delight. Sharon crouched beside her, laughing when a tiny rusty red rabbit tried to poke its pink nose through the mesh.

'I think this one likes you, Jessica. Isn't he sweet?'

'He's gorgeous,' the child whispered. She poked a finger through the mesh, laughing when the rabbit immediately tried to nibble it.

'Mind he doesn't bite, love,' the stallholder warned. 'He might think your finger is a nice tasty treat to eat. Here, let me get him out for you to hold.'

He lifted the rabbit out of its cage and settled him on Jessica's knee. Sharon felt a lump come to her throat when she saw the expression of bliss that crossed the little girl's face as she stroked the animal's silky fur.

'He's beautiful. Just feel how soft his fur is, Sharon,' Jessica whispered in an awestruck tone.

Sharon bent down and gently stroked the rabbit, smiling when his whiskers began to twitch as he sniffed her hand. 'Look, he's trying to decide if he likes me. Oops, I think he prefers you!'

Jessica laughed in delight when the tiny creature turned his back on Sharon and nestled into her arms. 'That's because he knows that I love him. Do you think Daddy will buy him for me, Sharon?'

'I don't know, sweetheart. You'll have to ask him. But maybe he'll decide that he's too busy to look after a rabbit,

so you mustn't be too disappointed if he says no,' she
warned, not wanting to raise the child's hopes.

'I can look after him myself! I got this book from the
library and it tells you all about what rabbits eat and how
to take care of them. All I need is a hutch for him to live
in and some straw and—'

'Hmm, sounds like somebody is doing some plotting,' a
deep voice remarked.

Sharon looked up, feeling her heart give the strangest
little jolt when she saw that Matt had returned. He looked
so big and handsome as he stood there, smiling down at
them, that it struck her how much she would enjoy having
him look at her like that more often. She could build a
whole future on a smile like that.

She rose to her feet abruptly, shocked at herself. She
barely knew this man and it was ridiculous to start fantas-
ising along those lines!

'I think Jessica has fallen in love with this little fellow,'
she quickly explained because she was afraid that he would
sense there was something wrong.

'You do surprise me,' he replied drolly. He looked at his
daughter and the sadness on his face at that moment made
Sharon's eyes mist with tears. 'She takes after her mother.
Claire was passionate about animals, too.'

Sharon didn't know what to say. It was strange because
she longed to find out more about his wife, yet hearing him
speak about the dead woman was too painful. It made her
realise that he might never get over Claire's death and that
idea appalled her.

Matt looked up and frowned when he caught sight of her
stricken expression. 'What's the matter?'

'I...I've just remembered that I'm supposed to be meeting a friend,' she lied, dredging up the first excuse she
could think of. It obviously worked because his mouth
thinned.

'And now we've made you late. I'm sorry. I never meant to delay you. Thanks again for looking after Jessica. I really appreciate it.'

He sounded so distant all of a sudden that Sharon's heart ached. She would have given anything to have explained that he had nothing to apologise for. However, that would have meant explaining about the lie she had told and there was no way that she could do that. How could she explain why it hurt to know that he was still in love with his wife when she didn't understand the reason herself?

'It was my pleasure,' she said instead, then turned to the little girl. 'I hope we meet again soon, Jessica.'

'Me, too. Maybe Sharon can come for tea one day, Daddy,' the child suggested hopefully.

'I'm sure Sharon is very busy, darling,' he replied, neither agreeing nor disagreeing. However, Sharon knew that he had no intention of issuing any such invitation. As far as Matt was concerned, this had been a one-off occasion, driven by necessity rather than choice. He wouldn't willingly involve her in his personal life again.

She fixed a smile to her mouth to stop him seeing how hurtful that thought was. 'I'd better be off, then. I'll see you next week.'

'Yes, and thanks again, Sharon,' he replied politely.

Sharon managed another smile but her heart was heavy as she made her way through the crowd that thronged the market square. Matt had made it clear that he intended to keep her at a distance and she had to accept that. However, it was less easy to understand why it should upset her. Matt was just someone she worked with so why did she hate the thought that he was deliberately shutting her out of his life?

'Man with severe chest pains—query possible heart attack. He's collapsed close to the fourteenth hole at Daleside Golf

Club. How long do you think it will take us to get there, Andy?'

Sharon waited while the pilot checked their bearings. They had been on their way back to base after transporting an injured motorist to hospital when a second call had come through. Although they had got to the motorist within ten minutes, he had died on the way to hospital and they were all feeling a bit dejected. Hopefully, this call would turn out better than the previous one, but there were no guarantees. By the very nature of their job they dealt with the most severely injured people, and the odds were usually stacked against them.

'Roughly ten minutes,' Andy finally announced.

'Right, I'll tell Mike.'

Matt relayed the information then settled back as the pilot turned the helicopter onto its new setting. It was a brilliantly sunny morning and the sun glared through the tinted Perspex windscreen as they altered course. Sharon felt in her pocket for her sunglasses then sighed when she remembered that she had left them in her locker in the rush to get out.

'Here, use mine.' Matt offered her his glasses, shaking his head when she started to refuse. 'I'm not getting the full glare of the sun from here. You need them more than I do, Sharon.'

He gave her one of his rare smiles and she quickly took the glasses, relieved to be able to hide behind their tinted lenses. She knew it was silly but she had found it impossible to stop thinking about him since their encounter in the market place. All weekend long she had found her thoughts returning to what had happened. It was as though that glimpse she'd had of his private life had heightened her interest.

'I bought Jess that rabbit, by the way,' he said right out of the blue. Sharon felt a frisson ripple down her spine as

she wondered if he had picked up on her thoughts somehow. She shot him a wary glance but there was nothing on
his face to indicate that he had.

'I expect she was pleased. I take it that she's been asking
for a rabbit for some time?' she said carefully. She wasn't
comfortable with the thought of *anyone* reading her
thoughts at the present time—least of all Matt.

'She's been pestering me for a dog, but it just isn't fea-
sible for us to have one so a rabbit is a compromise,' he
explained, then suddenly laughed. 'I don't know if you'll
be flattered but Jess has called it Sharon after you. She
seemed to think it was the perfect name even though I did
point out that it's a boy.'

Sharon couldn't help laughing. 'Well, it's different, I'll
say that. I just hope the poor creature doesn't get a complex!'

'A gender-bending bunny, eh?' Andy chipped in. 'It
could be something else for the press, Sharon. I wonder
what sort of headline they could come up with if they got
to know that you'd had a rabbit named in your honour?'

She knew that he was alluding to the newspaper article
and her heart sank. Nobody had mentioned it when she had
arrived at work that day, although there hadn't been much
chance because they had been called out almost immediately. However, she knew that if Andy had seen the photograph then the others would soon hear about it, and she
couldn't help wondering what Matt would say. Recalling
his comments at the time the picture was taken, she didn't
think it would go down too well.

'Who knows?' she said, then quickly changed the subject. 'How long before we get there?'

'Roughly five minutes. Let's hope that someone has had
the sense to put out a marker so that we can find them. The
fourteenth hole isn't the most accurate map reference I've
ever been given,' Andy replied dryly.

Sharon breathed a sigh of relief when he let the subject drop, but she wasn't blind to the frowning look Matt gave her. Fortunately, the golf course came into sight just then so they were too busy looking for where they were supposed to land for him to question her.

The golfer was in a pretty poor state. He was in a great deal of pain so Matt immediately set about administering a strong analgesic to make him more comfortable. Sharon set up the monitoring equipment so that they could get an accurate readout on what was happening while Matt followed up the painkillers with thrombolytic drugs to dissolve the blood clot that was blocking the man's artery.

Sharon knew that the sooner the patient was started on this treatment the greater his chances of recovery would be, but it was obvious from Matt's grim expression that it was going to be touch and go once again.

'Right, let's get that oxygen mask on him and get him to hospital a.s.a.p.,' he instructed tersely. He stood up while Sharon quickly fitted the mask over the golfer's nose and mouth.

'He is going to be all right? I mean, I'll have to phone his wife and tell her what's happened…'

The man's golfing partner looked dismayed at the prospect of having to be the bearer of bad news. Sharon saw Matt draw him to one side while she and Bert loaded the stretcher on board. She guessed that Matt was explaining how serious the man's condition was. It was an aspect of the job that was always difficult to deal with. They had a duty not to falsely raise people's hopes yet it wasn't easy to explain that they should be prepared for the worst.

They were in the air a few minutes later and heading for the nearest hospital. Sharon was monitoring the patient and it was obvious that his condition was deteriorating. Matt's expression was very tense as he kept watch over the portable ECG screen.

'I don't like the look of him at all,' Matt observed worriedly. 'He's very bradycardic.'

'He could have been suffering from coronary artery disease for some time,' Sharon replied, watching the slow, irregular heartbeat pattern that was being displayed on the monitor. 'He's definitely overweight, and from the look of those nicotine stains on his fingers, he's a heavy smoker, too.'

'A lethal combination.' Matt sighed. 'His friend told me that they'd only taken up golf a couple of months ago. They both work in an office and decided that they needed to get some exercise. Let's hope that the change in lifestyle hasn't come too late.'

The words seemed prophetic because they had just touched down when the man arrested.

'Let's get him out of here stat!' Matt flung open the door and jumped onto the landing pad before the engines had even stopped. There were staff from the A and E unit waiting for them, and they came racing over when they saw what was happening.

'Heart stopped just as we touched down,' he informed them crisply, turning to Sharon. 'Hand me the defibrillator and somebody start CPR!'

Two of the A and E staff rushed to assist. Sharon quickly unloaded the portable defibrillator and set it up. Although the hospital's own A and E unit would have a more sophisticated version of the machine, they couldn't afford to wait until they got the patient inside.

'Clear!' Matt applied the paddles to the man's chest and sent a jolt of electricity through his heart. 'No good. Let's give it another shot. Clear!'

Everyone stepped back once more while he tried a second time but there was still no result. Sharon felt her spirits sink as she wondered if all their hard work had been in vain. The prospect of losing another patient so early in the day didn't bear thinking about.

'One more try and let's hope it's third time lucky,' Matt declared with a trace of black humour. However, she knew that it was merely a cover for his true feelings and that he must be feeling as dejected as she was.

'Yes!' His shout of delight said it all as the man's heart suddenly started beating again. There was a burst of applause from the A and E staff and he stood up and took a bow, much to everyone's amusement. One of the nurses sighed as she passed Sharon on her way into the building.

'Lucky you! What I wouldn't give to trade places and do your job.'

Sharon laughed, although it was difficult to hide her irritation. It was obvious that the main attraction about her job was the chance to work with Matt.

'It isn't all roses,' she said rather too sharply.

'Show me a job that is,' the nurse replied, giving her an old-fashioned look. 'Anyway, I didn't mean to step on your toes. Sorry.'

She didn't say anything more as she hurried after her colleagues. Sharon felt her cheeks suffuse with colour when she realised that she had given the other woman the totally wrong impression. She had no claim on Matt and she certainly shouldn't have made it appear that she had.

'Well, let's hope that did the trick...' Matt stopped what he was saying and looked at her curiously. 'Are you all right, Sharon? You look upset.' He suddenly sighed. 'I know it isn't easy when you lose a patient, but you have to try to be positive and think about the lives you save rather than the ones you don't.'

His sympathy was so unexpected that she raised startled eyes to his face. 'Is that what you do?'

'Of course. Why, didn't you imagine that it upsets me when we have a patient die like the one this morning?' He shrugged as he turned to board the helicopter. 'I wouldn't be in this job if I didn't care.'

'I know that!' She stopped him as he was about to move away. 'I know that you care, Matt. What I don't understand is why you are at such pains to hide your feelings.'

'I don't know what you mean—' he began, but she didn't let him finish.

'Of course you do! You hide behind the mask of professionalism all the time. Would it be such a crime to let down your guard occasionally?' She sighed when he looked at her. 'It seems to me that you deliberately distance yourself from people and I can't understand it.'

'Interesting though this discussion is, I'm afraid that we don't have the time to pursue it.' His tone was icy, telling her clearly that she had overstepped the boundaries. 'We have work to do so let's concentrate on that.'

He climbed on board without another word. Bert was already strapped in his seat and he said something to her as she took her place. Sharon responded automatically but her mind wasn't on the conversation. Matt's instant withdrawal when she had dared to pass a personal comment was going to haunt her for a long time to come.

They arrived back at base shortly before lunch. Sharon hung her helmet on its peg and went to the staffroom. She had brought sandwiches with her and had decided to eat them outside. There was a small garden at the rear of the building—a bit straggly and overgrown but there was a bench there where she could sit. Frankly, she felt like being on her own for a while to unwind after the rigours of the morning. However, when she entered the staffroom she found everyone waiting for her.

'Here she is, our very own pin-up! Ladies and gentlemen, I give you the lovely Sharon Lennard.'

She groaned when Mike held up a copy of the weekly paper. 'I was hoping you lot hadn't seen that!'

'No chance,' he assured her. 'Anyway, I don't know why you want to hide it from us. It's a great photo and should do wonders for our image, although I must say that I think a photo of a particularly dashing radio operator could be rather a draw for the ladies…'

Sharon laughed as a chorus of boos greeted that suggestion. 'Why do I get the feeling that your colleagues don't agree with you? Some of us obviously have what it takes and others don't. It's one of those sad facts of life that one has to accept.'

'I always thought this crowd was lacking in taste,' Mike retorted. 'Oh, before I forget, there was a phone call for you this morning. A reporter from one of the nationals wants an interview. Looks like you could find yourself making the headlines countrywide.'

'No way!' she declared. 'If he rings again just tell him thanks but, no, thanks, will you? I'm not interested in publicity, only in doing my job.'

He sighed. 'OK, will do. But it would have been nice if I'd been able to tell my friends that I knew you before you were famous.'

Sharon rolled her eyes as he moved away. Famous, indeed!

She collected her lunch then went outside. The garden was even more overgrown than she had realised and she had to trample a path to reach the bench. However, it was worth it just to be out in the fresh air. She ate her sandwiches then settled back to enjoy the rest of her lunch break. The station backed onto fields and the only sound to disturb the peace was coming from a tractor ploughing in the distance. She was almost asleep when she heard the back door slam and looked round to see Matt heading her way.

'Sorry. I didn't mean to disturb you,' he apologised, stopping by the bench. He held up a plastic carrier bag and grimaced. 'I promised Jessica that I would bring some dandelion leaves home for the other Sharon.'

She chuckled at that. 'This could get very confusing! How about making me Sharon mark one and the rabbit mark two?'

'Or maybe I could persuade Jess to choose another name?' he replied with an engaging grin that made her breath catch. 'Whatever happened to proper rabbit names like Flopsy and Mopsy?'

'Not sophisticated enough. I have a neighbour who has called her cats Desdemona and Othello,' she told him, determined not to let him see the effect he'd had on her. 'It caused quite a stir at first when she used to come out each night and call them in for their supper.'

Matt laughed out loud. 'I can imagine! Obviously, I'm completely out of touch when it comes to naming pets.'

He made his way through the long grass and bent down by the wall and began rapidly filling the carrier bag with dandelion leaves. 'That should do for now,' he declared, knotting the top of the bag. 'I can pick some more another day.'

'Don't you have a garden at home?' she asked curiously. 'Or is it the kind of garden where no weeds dare to sprout because you instantly annihilate them?'

'I wish! I've fought many a losing battle with weeds in my time,' he admitted, sitting down on the end of the bench. 'Luckily, I don't have that problem now because I've had most of the garden paved. It's easier for Jess to get around, you see. Her chair kept getting stuck if it had been raining and the ground was wet.'

'Sounds like it was a good idea, although poor little Sharon rabbit might not agree,' she said lightly, thinking that it was yet another problem she had never given any thought to.

'Oh, we've still got a bit of grass left and a lot of plants in the borders so it isn't too bleak. However, Jess found it frustrating always having to ask someone to help her so it seemed like a good idea. There are enough restrictions on what she can do without making her life even more difficult.'

'It can't be easy, coping with a child who has mobility problems,' she observed quietly. 'I hadn't realised the difficulties parents must face until last Saturday. Just performing everyday tasks like shopping must need to be planned in advance.'

'Tell me about it!' He sighed heavily. 'I'm on a committee that's pushing for easier access for the disabled. There are still a lot of public buildings in the town which are impossible to enter for anyone in a wheelchair. Despite the recent laws that have been passed, there are still far too many obstacles for the disabled to contend with. It costs money to build ramps and widen doors, you see.'

'It must be a constant headache. The trouble is that most people, like me, don't appreciate the difficulties involved. It isn't that we're uncaring—it's just that unless you're faced with the problem on a personal level then you don't give it much thought.'

'It's only natural, isn't it? Thankfully, most people will never find themselves in the position Jessica is in.'

'Is there any chance at all that she will walk again?' she asked quietly, wondering if she might be overstepping the boundaries once more. She was surprised that Matt had opened up to this extent—surprised and *pleased*. Maybe it was foolish to see it as a sign that he was willing to lower his guard a little, but she couldn't help it.

'None. Her spinal cord was severed in the accident that killed her mother. Unless there are tremendous advances made in neurological research, she will never regain full mobility.'

Her heart ached when she heard the pain in his voice. 'It must have been a nightmare for you. Having to cope with your wife's death would have been hard enough, but having to deal with Jessica's injuries must have made the situation doubly difficult.'

'It hasn't been easy, although I like to think that we are over the worst now. At one point I couldn't envisage us ever getting back any degree of normality into our lives. We have bad days, of course. But most of the time Jess and I muddle through.'

He stared across the garden. Sharon knew that he must be thinking about all the changes that had occurred in his life. She longed to offer her help but she knew that he would reject it. Matt might have unbent this far but there was a point beyond which he wasn't prepared to go.

She stood up, suddenly wanting to escape from a situation she was finding it increasingly hard to deal with. What was the point of upsetting herself because he didn't want her help? They were just two people who worked together and she had to remember that.

'I'd better get ready in case we have any more calls,' she explained when he looked round.

'Me, too.' He picked up the bag of dandelion leaves and led the way back to the building, pausing politely to hold the door open for her. Mike was coming along the corridor and he waved to her.

'I was just coming to find you, Sharon. That reporter's on the phone again. He's very insistent about wanting to speak to you.'

'What's this all about?' Matt asked immediately. His face darkened when Mike cheerfully explained about the article in the local paper. He turned to Sharon and she was chilled by the expression in his eyes.

'I would appreciate it if you told that reporter not to phone you here again. The last thing we need is the press hanging around here, making a nuisance of themselves.'

'I didn't ask him to phone…' she began, but Matt had already turned to go into his office.

Mike grimaced. 'Sorry. I didn't mean to drop you in it like that. Me and my big mouth, eh?'

'It wasn't your fault,' she assured him. 'Anyway, would you just tell the reporter that I'm not interested and that I won't change my mind.'

'Will do. I suppose it's understandable if Matt's wary of the press. I believe they hounded him after his wife died. I've a friend who works in the hospital where he worked, and she told me that there were reporters all over the place wanting to interview him after the accident.' Mike shook his head. 'They didn't make any allowance for the fact that the poor guy's life had been ripped apart. They just wanted a story.'

Sharon sighed as Mike hurried off. No wonder Matt had been annoyed. If only he'd given her a chance to explain that she had no intention of encouraging the journalist.

She hesitated, wondering if she should speak to him and try to clear up the misunderstanding. But a glance at the closed door to his office made up her mind. As far as Matt was concerned, the subject was closed. The fact that it hurt to know that the incident wouldn't have improved his opinion of her was her problem.

They were just two people who worked together, she reminded herself as she went to the staffroom. Maybe she should make a sign and tape it to her locker door because it was proving surprisingly difficult to keep it in mind!

CHAPTER FOUR

IT WAS the busiest day that Sharon had known since starting work with the air ambulance service. They had three more calls that afternoon and by the end of her shift she was glad to hand over to the other team. Beth Maguire grimaced when she saw the list of calls they had attended.

'Wow! Looks like a fun day was had by all. Still, it's better than sitting around, waiting for something to happen, isn't it? I get a bit twitchy with nothing to do.'

'Well, if it keeps on the way it's been going all day then you certainly won't have a chance to get bored,' Sharon assured her. 'Frankly, I'm beat. I intend to go home and put my feet up for the rest of the night!'

'Lucky you!' Beth laughed. 'When I get in I usually have to start on the housework. Take my advice, Sharon, and don't have kids—they make a lot of work!'

'I bet you wouldn't swop them,' Sharon retorted.

'Ask me that on a day when my youngest is playing up.' Beth rolled her eyes comically. 'I'd give him away for free never mind swop him! Wait till you have kids of your own then you'll understand what I mean.'

Sharon laughed. 'Not much chance of that at the moment, I can assure you!'

'Aren't you going out with anyone?' Beth was obviously eager to hear more.

'I'm afraid not. I love kids, though, and definitely want to have them at some point. However, seeing as I haven't yet found the right man, children come way down my list of priorities at the moment,' she explained. She glanced round when she heard footsteps and felt her smile fade when she saw Matt. He gave them a brief nod then carried on down the corridor and left the building.

'Oh, well, there's plenty of time.' Beth grimaced. 'And I don't know why I'm complaining. When I compare my life to what Matt has to contend with it makes me realise how lucky I am. At least I have Dave to share the load, but Matt has nobody.'

'He's not met anyone since his wife died, then?' Sharon asked curiously.

'I don't think so. I've certainly never heard him mention another woman. But you know Matt, he isn't one to talk about his private life.'

They parted company after that—Beth went into the staffroom while Sharon went outside and got into her car. Funnily enough, it had never occurred to her before that Matt might have someone else in his life. Now she found that she couldn't get the idea out of her head. He was a very attractive man and there must be a lot of women who would want to share his life. Or had he ruled out the possibility of another relationship because he was still in love with his wife?

She sighed when she realised that once again her thoughts were full of him. Matt wouldn't thank her for spending so much time worrying about his affairs!

Sharon drove towards town, debating whether she should stop on the way home to buy a take-away. It had been a hectic day and she didn't feel like cooking when she got in. There was a Chinese restaurant on the outskirts of the town that did meals to take out so she headed that way. However, she had gone no more than a few hundred yards when she spotted Matt's car pulled up at the side of the road with steam gushing out of its bonnet.

She drew up behind it and climbed out. 'What's happened?'

'Radiator must have sprung a leak. I noticed that the

engine was overheating, which is why I stopped.' He moved her out of the way as another cloud of steam gushed out. 'Careful, it's hot!'

'What are you going to do now?' she asked in concern.

'There's not much I can do except arrange for the garage to collect it.' He checked his watch and sighed. 'Why did it have to happen tonight of all nights? I promised Jess that I would take her to the cinema and she's going to be so disappointed that we won't be able to go. We usually go to the early show so that she's not too late getting to bed, but we'll never make it in time now.'

'Maybe I could give you a lift?' Sharon offered immediately. She sensed that he was going to refuse and hurried on. 'The cinema is on my way home so it isn't any trouble and you can get a taxi home from there afterwards.'

'Well, if you're sure...' It was obvious that he was torn between a desire not to disappoint his daughter and reluctance to accept her help. However, in the end his daughter's needs won. 'Thanks, Sharon. It's really good of you to offer.'

He closed the car's bonnet and locked the doors then got into her car. Sharon started the engine, barely able to contain the feeling of happiness fizzing inside her. That Matt had accepted her offer of help seemed like such a breakthrough...

She bit back a sigh. Steady, girl! Don't get carried away. He might have accepted a lift but that was all.

'If you turn left when you come to the crossroads, I live halfway down that road,' he explained when they reached the town centre. Sharon nodded, concentrating on driving them safely through the rush hour traffic. She drew up outside a solid-looking, detached house and switched off the engine, wondering if she should offer to wait in the car. However, the decision was taken from her when Jessica

suddenly appeared at the gate. The little girl's face lit up
as soon as she saw her.

'Have you come to see my rabbit?' she demanded eagerly as Sharon got out to speak to her.

'Actually, I was giving your daddy a lift home because
his car has broken down. But I would love to see him if it
isn't too much trouble,' she told her.

'Of course not! He's in the back garden. Come along
and I'll show you.'

Jessica swung her wheelchair around and disappeared
round the side of the house. Sharon looked at Matt, not
wanting to appear too presumptuous, but he just grinned.

'Go and have a look. Jess will be so disappointed if you
don't admire him.'

She smiled back, feeling happier once she knew that he
didn't think she was encroaching on his privacy. She followed the path and found Jessica waiting for her beside a
brand-new hutch. She couldn't help chuckling when she
saw the sign fixed to its door announcing to the world that
the rabbit was called Sharon.

'Daddy told me that you'd decided to name him after
me,' she observed lightly, bending down to look at her
namesake.

'You don't mind, do you?' Jessica said quickly. 'I know
he's a boy and you're a girl but his fur is the same colour
as your hair, you see.'

'Perfectly logical, isn't it?' Matt observed so dryly that
she was hard pressed not to laugh.

'It is. And of course I don't mind, sweetheart. I think it's
a lovely idea. I've never had a rabbit named after me before
so I shall take it as a compliment.'

'I knew you'd be pleased,' the little girl stated with total
conviction. 'Didn't I tell you that Sharon wouldn't mind,
Daddy?'

'You did indeed!' Matt laughed as he bent and hugged

her. Once again Sharon was deeply touched by his obvious love for the child. It brought it home to her all the more sharply what he was denying himself. Deep down Matt was a warm and loving man yet he seemed determined to suppress his own feelings.

'Right, I'd better go and tell Mrs Gregson that I'm back so she can get off home. Then I'll phone the garage and ask them to pick up the car.'

Sharon looked at him curiously. 'Mrs Gregson?'

'She looks after Jessica while I'm at work,' he explained.

'You don't have live-in help, then?' she asked, skirting delicately around the question of there being another woman in his life.

'No. I prefer to take care of Jess myself, although obviously I have to make provision for the times when I'm working. However, all things considered, we manage quite well, don't we, sprog?'

'Uh-huh, except that you can't make cakes, Daddy. Sarah's mummy makes lots and *lots* of cakes, but you don't know how to make them.' Jessica turned eagerly to her. 'Can you make cakes, Sharon? Will you show me if you can?'

'I'm sure that Sharon has far more important things to do than teach you how to bake,' Matt said before Sharon had a chance to answer. He sighed when he saw his daughter's crestfallen expression. 'Why don't you ask Mrs Gregson to help you make some?'

'I did, but she said that she wasn't paid to do baking,' the child muttered.

Sharon saw his mouth thin and understood why he was annoyed. Surely it wouldn't have been that much trouble for the woman to show Jessica how to bake?

It was on the tip of her tongue to tell the little girl that she would be happy to teach her but she knew it would be the wrong thing to do. Matt wouldn't appreciate her forcing her help on him.

Thankfully, Jessica soon cheered up, and while Matt went inside she showed Sharon all the things she had bought for the rabbit. She even insisted on lifting him out of his hutch so that Sharon could watch her brush him.

It was obvious that she was thrilled about taking care of the little creature and Sharon couldn't help thinking what a good idea it was to give her the responsibility. There was a lot more to being a good parent than just caring for a child's physical well-being, not that Matt needed any pointers in that direction.

He came back a short time later and helped Jessica put the rabbit back in his hutch. Glancing at his watch, he turned to Sharon. 'Are you sure you don't mind dropping us off? I don't want to spoil your evening.'

'You aren't. My date will wait,' she said jokingly, following Jessica down the path.

'You should have said that you had a date—' he began, then frowned when she laughed. 'What's so funny?'

'My *date* is with myself. The only plans I have for the evening are to buy a take-away and eat it in front of the television.'

'I see.' He gave a sudden laugh but she wasn't deaf to the curiosity it held. 'I can't imagine it's something you do very often. I expect it makes a pleasant change to have a night in for once.'

'I hate to disappoint you, but I don't lead a hectic social life. In fact, I can honestly say that I can't remember the last time I went out at night.'

'Really?' He stopped and stared at her in surprise. 'I find that very hard to believe, quite frankly. Is there a reason for it?'

'I didn't have time for a social life while I was looking after my father,' she explained lightly, not wanting him to think that she was inviting sympathy. 'It was difficult to leave the house for any length of time so I lost touch with all but a few really close friends.'

'I hadn't realised. Oh, I knew from your job application that the reason you left London was because your father had suffered a stroke, but I hadn't realised that you were his sole carer.'

'My mother died ten years ago and I don't have any sisters or brothers. There was only me to look after Dad and I was happy to do it.'

'Not many women of your age would put their lives on hold like that,' he observed quietly.

'Oh, I disagree. A lot of people would have done what I did.' Her tone was deliberately upbeat because she didn't want him thinking that she resented giving up a year of her life. She had done it out of love for her father and the fact that his last days had been so happy had made it all worthwhile.

'Anyway, there's plenty of time to rebuild my social life. I'm hardly over the hill yet so there's plenty of time to do all the things I want to do!'

'Of course,' he agreed in a tone that made her wonder what he was thinking. She shot him an uncertain look but he had turned to reply to something Jessica had said to him. Sharon sighed as she followed them out to the street. She really must stop trying to analyse everything he said!

Jessica was really excited at the prospect of travelling in a strange car. She chattered away while Matt lifted her into the rear seat and fastened her seat belt. He rolled his eyes as he deftly collapsed her wheelchair and carried it round to the boot.

'She's on a real high, I'm afraid. Your ears will be ringing from all her chatter!'

Sharon laughed as she helped him stow the chair into the boot. It was a tight squeeze because her car wasn't nearly as roomy as his was. 'I can stand it. I've developed a tolerance for noise over the years with spending most of my time roaring up and down city streets.'

'You're going to need it!' he declared pithily, slamming the boot lid.

It turned out that he was right because Jessica never stopped talking all the way to the cinema. Sharon enjoyed the lively conversation, however. She had spent such a lot of time on her own that it was a treat to have such lively company. She felt quite sorry when she drew up in front of the cinema. The prospect of another night in front of the television suddenly didn't seem nearly as appealing as it had done.

Matt quickly unloaded the wheelchair and got Jessica settled. He turned to Sharon, a smile lighting his handsome face. 'Thank you so much for taking the time to drive us here tonight...'

He stopped when Jessica tugged on his sleeve, and bent down so that she could whisper something in his ear. Sharon saw him shake his head and she frowned as she wondered what was going on.

'Please, Daddy!' Jessica implored, and Matt sighed. Straightening, he turned to Sharon with a rueful smile. 'I know this is a huge imposition but would you like to stay and watch the film with us? Jessica would be thrilled if you'd agree.'

'Well, I'm not sure—' she began, not wanting to foist herself onto him when it was obvious that it had been the child's idea.

'I'd like you to stay as well, Sharon. Please, say that you will.'

Perhaps she could have refused the child's request but she certainly couldn't refuse his. She took a deep breath to quieten the noisy pounding of her heart. It was silly to read too much into the invitation but she couldn't help it. That

Matt had unbent enough to actually want her company seemed like a huge step forward.

'Then, yes, thank you. I'd love to stay.'

'Brill!' Jessica gave a whoop of delight then headed towards the entrance at a rate of knots. Matt hurried after her, leaving Sharon to follow at a more sedate pace. He helped Jessica up the ramp then turned to smile at her. Sharon felt her heart lift. If it was a mistake to get more deeply involved in his affairs then it certainly didn't feel like it at that moment!

'That was brilliant!'

Jessica sounded decidedly awestruck when they left the cinema a couple of hours later. She had been completely enthralled by the film they had seen. Sharon had enjoyed it, too, although she knew that part of her pleasure stemmed from knowing that the little girl was having such a good time.

'Can we go for a pizza now?' Jessica clamoured as they made for the exit. There was quite a large crowd leaving at the same time and they had to stop to let people pass before they could manoeuvre her chair down the ramp.

Sharon saw a woman glance at Jessica then look quickly away, and wondered if it was something that happened often. She couldn't help thinking how hurtful it must be for the child to be treated like an oddity. Although Jessica couldn't walk, there was nothing wrong with her mind and she must be aware of the attention she attracted. She felt an unexpected surge of protectiveness for the little girl and was glad that Matt couldn't read her mind because she doubted whether he would appreciate her feeling that way.

'Of course we can,' he assured her. 'I promised you a pizza and I never go back on a promise, do I?'

'No.' Jessica hugged herself with glee as they set off across the car park. The cinema was part of a new leisure

complex and there were several fast-food restaurants dotted
about. Sharon realised that she had been automatically included in their plans for the after-film treat so she walked
beside Jessica's chair, listening to the little girl excitedly
chattering away about the film.

Matt paused when they reached the restaurant and his
eyes held a hint of amusement as she reached past him to
open the door. 'Don't worry, she does stop talking while
she's eating, so your ears will get a rest.'

Sharon chuckled. 'I'll believe that when it happens.'

'I don't blame you!' he replied, deftly manoeuvring the
chair into the restaurant. There was a reception desk just
inside the foyer so they waited there to be seated. A lot of
cinema-goers must have had the same idea as they'd had
because the place was packed. Sharon frowned as she
looked round. The only free table was tucked right into a
corner and it could be a bit tricky to get Jessica's wheelchair over to it.

'I'm sorry but we don't have room tonight for a wheelchair.' The hostess gave them a dismissive smile then beck-
oned to the people behind them in the queue. Sharon saw
Matt's expression darken as she led the family to the last
free table and got them seated.

'Can't we have a pizza, then, Daddy?' Jessica asked,
looking crestfallen as she watched the other children take
their places.

'We might have to wait for a table nearer to the door,'
he explained gently. Sharon saw him beckon the hostess
but she ignored him. Twice more he tried to attract her
attention and each time the woman pretended not to notice.
Sharon could tell that he was growing increasingly annoyed
and could appreciate why. It was blatant discrimination and
she would never have believed it happened if she hadn't
witnessed it with her own eyes.

'I think they're rather busy tonight, don't you, Sharon?'

He turned to her and she understood at once what he was trying to do. Matt didn't want his daughter to suspect that the reason they were being ignored was because of her. 'How about getting that take-away you mentioned instead?'

'Sounds like a good idea to me,' she said at once. She smiled at Jessica, feeling her heart ache when she saw the child's disappointment.

'How about a Chinese meal instead of pizza, sweetheart? We could have fortune cookies as well, which would be fun.'

'What are they?' the little girl asked at once. She seemed to brighten up after Sharon had explained that each cookie contained a slip of paper with a fortune written on it. 'Can we have some? Really? One for you and one for Daddy and one for me?'

'Of course we can!' Sharon bent and hugged her. 'Who needs pizza when you can have fortune cookies?'

Jessica laughed. She seemed to have got over her disappointment. However, it was obvious that Matt was still angry, even though he took care to hide his feelings from the child.

'We don't!' He turned to Sharon and silently mouthed the words 'Thank you.' Then he quickly steered Jessica's chair out through the door.

He got her settled in the car then drew Sharon to one side.

'I'm just going back to have a word with the manager at that pizza place. I don't intend to let them get away with treating people like that. Would you mind staying here with Jess? It shouldn't take long.'

'Of course not.' She sighed as she watched him striding across the car park. As if he didn't have enough to worry about. However, she agreed wholeheartedly that he shouldn't let the incident pass. The sooner people were made to understand that they couldn't treat the disabled like second-class citizens, the better for everyone.

He came back about ten minutes later and got into the car. Sharon started the engine then glanced at him. 'OK?'

'Fine. I don't think there will be any problems there in the future. It's amazing how quickly people realise that they need to change their attitude when you explain what it could cost them,' he said dryly.

'But sad that you have to do it in the first place,' she observed, glancing in the mirror at Jessica.

He reached over and squeezed her hand. 'Don't let it upset you, Sharon.'

He let go of her hand and turned to speak to Jessica. Sharon took a deep breath but if any air got into her body then it certainly didn't reach her lungs. She set off towards the Chinese restaurant, trying her hardest to put what had happened into perspective. However, it wasn't easy to explain why her fingers were tingling from that brief contact.

She glanced sideways and felt a rush of warmth invade her when Matt turned and smiled at her. Suddenly, it felt as though in that instant her whole life had shifted from the path she had chosen. She didn't need a fortune cookie to tell her that her future was going to be linked to this man's.

'Asleep at last!' Matt flopped down on the sofa and cupped a hand to his ear. 'Listen.'

Sharon frowned as she did as he'd said. The evening had flown past since they had got back to Matt's house. Jessica had been thrilled with the bag of fortune cookies and had insisted on doling them out so that they each had some. However, Matt had been firm and had insisted that she must wait until after they'd eaten before reading the messages they had contained.

Once the food had been eaten they had each broken open their cookies and let Jessica read their fortunes. There had been a lot of laughter as the child had solemnly advised them about journeys they were going to make and people they would meet. It had been a bit of harmless fun and Sharon had enjoyed it, especially as there had been no reference to any huge changes suddenly occurring in her life. Frankly, she intended to get that crazy notion out of her head as fast as she could!

'I can't hear anything,' she said at last, frowning.

'Exactly. Isn't it wonderful? Peace, perfect peace!'

The rueful note in his voice made her laugh. 'You know very well that you would worry if Jessica was too quiet.'

'I know, I know!' He held up his hands. 'I admit it, but that doesn't mean I can't make the most of it on occasion. That child could talk the hind leg off a donkey!'

'Most little girls can. My father used to call me Sharon Chatterbox when I was Jessica's age. I expect he felt the same as you do—that silence is golden at times.'

'A man after my own heart. I'm sure we would have got on well if we'd met.' He suddenly sighed. 'Thanks for tonight, Sharon. I really appreciate everything you did. I just hope that you didn't think I was putting on you.'

'Of course not! I enjoyed it myself, apart from that episode at the pizza restaurant. Thank heavens Jessica didn't realise what was going on.'

'But it won't always be like that, I'm afraid. At some point she's going to recognise that the reason she can't do all the things other people do isn't solely because of her physical handicap.' His tone was harsh all of a sudden. Sharon sensed that this was something that worried him a lot.

'Sometimes it's down to ignorance, which is bad enough, but a lot of the time it's simply because people can't be bothered to make provision for the less able members of society.'

'It must be very difficult,' she said softly. 'You're bound

to feel very protective towards Jessica, but you must know that you could be doing more harm than good by shielding her from any unpleasantness.'

'That's exactly right. At some point she has to learn how to deal with both prejudice and ignorance, but she's only a child yet. She's been through so much already that I feel that I want to protect her for as long as possible.' He sighed as he stared at the ceiling. 'I'm just hoping that I can get the right balance eventually.'

'You will.' Sharon smiled when he looked at her. 'It's obvious that you're a wonderful father, Matt. Jessica is so lucky to have you.'

'Maybe. But it doesn't make up for the fact that she doesn't have a mother, does it? I can never do the things for her that Claire would have done. Claire was a wonderful mother and it breaks my heart to think about what Jessica is missing by not having her around.'

'Maybe you'll meet someone else one day and marry again,' she suggested but he shook his head.

'I'm not interested in getting married again. My only concern is to take care of Jessica to the very best of my ability. Nothing else matters apart from that.'

'But surely you deserve a life of your own? You're a young man, Matt, and it's wrong to rule out the chance of finding personal happiness again!'

She couldn't hide her dismay and she heard him sigh. 'I don't have the time or the inclination for another relationship. I have enough to do with work and taking care of Jess.'

'But if you met someone else then you could share Jessica's care. It would take some of the burden off you,' she insisted, wanting to convince him.

'By offloading it onto someone else, you mean? That wouldn't be fair. Jessica is my daughter and it is up to me to take care of her.'

He took a deep breath and she saw an expression of intense pain cross his face. 'It's the very least I can do considering that I'm responsible for what happened to her and her mother.'

CHAPTER FIVE

'WHAT do you mean, that you were responsible? I thought Jessica and her mother were involved in an accident?' Sharon could hear the shock in her voice although it was understandable in the circumstances.

'They were. A van ran out of control and mounted the pavement. It turned out that the driver had suffered a heart attack at the wheel.' Matt's tone was clipped, but she guessed that the only way he could speak about the tragedy was by keeping his emotions in check.

'There were a number of casualties, although Claire and Jessica were the most severely injured.' He stood up abruptly. 'The police told me that according to some witnesses Claire had tried to push Jess out of the way instead of jumping clear herself. That was typical of her. She wouldn't have given any thought for her own safety.'

He gave Sharon a sad little smile then continued in the same flat tone. 'The worst thing is that they shouldn't have been in town at that time of the day. Claire had taken Jess into town after school for some new shoes and had asked me to collect them on my way home. I was working in the casualty unit at the Royal at the time and had to drive through town to get home.

'We arranged to meet outside the shop at five o'clock but I got held up. Oh, it wasn't anything urgent, just a fracture that the junior houseman was having trouble with, so I stayed behind to help. If I hadn't done so then Claire and Jessica wouldn't have been there when the van ran into the crowd.'

Sharon didn't know what to say. Anything would sound

trite. It wasn't Matt's fault that he had been delayed but she knew that he didn't see it that way.

Her eyes filled with tears when she realised how hard it must have been for him since the accident, coping with his own misplaced sense of guilt as well as his grief. He must have tortured himself with the thought that the tragedy might not have happened if he'd been there on time.

'Sharon?'

She heard the puzzlement in his voice and jumped to her feet, not wanting him to see that she was upset. It wouldn't help to make him feel guilty about that as well. 'I...I'd better go...'

'I'm sorry. I didn't mean to upset you.' His voice grated with emotion all of a sudden and the tears spilled down her cheeks. It wasn't that Matt didn't feel but that he felt too much, and it hurt unbearably to know how difficult it must be for him to subjugate his own emotions so that he could get on with bringing up his daughter.

'It doesn't matter. I'm just being silly,' she said, hunting a tissue from her pocket and wiping her eyes. 'I'm sorry, Matt. I didn't mean to remind you of what happened.'

'It's me who should apologise. I rarely talk about Claire's death so I'm a little surprised that I poured out the whole tale like that. I didn't intend to.'

'I realise that.' She smiled sadly. 'You're a very private person, aren't you? But sometimes it helps to talk. You can't keep everything bottled up inside you. The one thing you must get out of your head, though, is that you were in any way to blame for what happened. It wasn't your fault. It was a tragic accident.'

'Perhaps.' He gave a slight shrug. 'Anyway, thanks for listening, Sharon. I appreciate it, and everything else you've done tonight.'

It was a dismissal and she didn't make the mistake of not seeing it for what it was. Matt was politely telling her that the evening had come to an end. He was probably regretting having opened up to her, if the truth be told.

Had her assurances that he hadn't been at fault helped ease his mind? she wondered. She doubted it and it hurt to know that there wasn't anything she could do to help him.

She made her way to the door, almost as anxious as he was to bring the evening to a close. It was pointless getting upset because Matt didn't want her help. She paused on the step, wondering if she should reassure him that she wouldn't mention their conversation to anyone. She would hate him to think that she might be tempted to gossip.

'Look, Matt, if you're worried about me saying anything to the others...' she began, then stopped when something caught her eye. It was a clear night, a full moon lighting the front garden as clearly as though it were day, which was why she had spotted the rabbit hopping across the lawn. 'Isn't that Jessica's rabbit?'

'If it isn't then it must have a twin brother,' he said grimly, making a dive for the tiny creature, which promptly hopped under a bush.

Sharon chuckled as she went to help him. 'Doesn't look too eager to be caught, does he?'

'You can say that again!' Matt lunged sideways as the rabbit made another bid for freedom. This time he actually managed to get his hands around the creature before it wriggled through his fingers. With a disdainful bob of its tail, it shot towards the hedge.

'Stop it!' he yelled. 'If it gets out into the road then we'll never catch it.'

Sharon made a running dive across the grass, landing on her knees in front of the rabbit. She quickly scooped him up and held grimly onto him. 'Got him!'

'Well done! Ever thought of trying for the England rugby squad?' Matt asked teasingly. 'They could do with a few players of your calibre.'

She laughed as she followed him to the back garden. 'I'll stick to medicine, thank you. I can live without having permanently bruised knees.'

He shot a rueful glance at her dirty jeans. 'I hope you didn't hurt yourself. That was some dive you took.'

'I'll survive,' she assured him, bending to pop the rabbit back inside his hutch. Matt crouched down and sighed as he tested the latch on the door.

'It looks as though it's worked itself loose. I'd better find a screwdriver and tighten it up otherwise Sharon mark two will be heading off again for pastures greener the minute our backs are turned.'

'I'll stay here and stand guard,' she told him as he straightened. 'Don't worry, this bunny isn't going *anywhere* else tonight!'

'Thanks. I don't think I could face Jessica if he disappeared. She's totally besotted with him. I'll go and find that screwdriver.'

He hurried inside the house while Sharon kept watch over the hutch. He came back a few minutes later and swiftly tightened the screws so that the latch wouldn't work free again.

'That should do it,' he declared, offering her a hand to help her to her feet. Sharon wasn't sure what happened next, whether it was the fact that her knees were stiff from crouching down, but all of a sudden she felt herself stumble.

'Careful!' Matt's arms came around her as she lurched forwards. Sharon found herself unexpectedly pressed against the hard wall of his chest and her heart seemed to come to a dead stop. She couldn't seem to think let alone move as her senses were suddenly swamped by his nearness.

When she breathed in she could smell the clean fragrance of his skin, and when she moved slightly she could feel the tautness of his body pressing against the softness of hers. She could even hear his heart beating and it seemed so intimate to be able to hear it that she shivered. Never had she been so aware of another human being as she was of Matt at that moment.

'Sharon?'

There was an oddly tentative note in his voice when he said her name. It shocked her to hear it because the last word she would have used to describe him was tentative. Matt was always so in control both of himself and his emotions that her eyes rose to his in bewilderment.

He uttered something rough under his breath yet she knew in her heart that it was surprise and not anger that had prompted it. That shocked her even more. Matt wasn't the kind of man who let life throw surprises at him. His life was too ordered, too regulated, too...

She couldn't contain the murmur that escaped her when his mouth found hers. Shock flooded through her but it was followed so swiftly by other emotions that it barely had a chance to register. It wasn't the first time she had been kissed so passionately, but it was the first time her own passion had been aroused so completely. It made all the other kisses she had shared with other men seem meaningless.

She kissed him back, wrapping her arms around his neck to draw him closer, murmuring again when his tongue slid into her mouth and met hers. Matt kissed her with a rawness and depth of emotion that left her aching when he finally raised his head. He seemed to have touched something deep inside her, unlocked feelings that she hadn't known she possessed. It must have been obvious how shaken she was by what had happened because she felt him go tense.

'I'm sorry. I shouldn't have—' he began.

'Don't!' She put her hand across his mouth, not wanting

to hear any more. She couldn't bear to have something so special spoiled by an apology. 'There's nothing to apologise for. If…if I hadn't wanted you to kiss me I would have said so.'

His eyes glittered and for a moment she wondered if he was going to take her back into his arms. She had already started to lean towards him when he abruptly let her go. 'Then all I shall say is that it won't happen again, Sharon. I wouldn't want to compromise our working relationship.'

'Oh, heaven forbid! It would be awful if you did that, wouldn't it?' She gave a brittle laugh, bitterly hurt by his attitude. 'Don't worry, Matt. I don't feel the least bit *compromised*, I can assure you. Let's just put it down to a moment of madness, shall we? And leave it at that.'

'Sharon!' He took a step towards her then stopped and took a deep breath. It was obvious that he was making an effort to collect himself and equally obvious that he had succeeded when his face smoothed into its customary bland expression.

'You're right. It has been a stressful day, one way and another. It's no wonder that we both acted out of character just now.'

Maybe it *had* been a momentary lapse on his behalf but that didn't alter the fact that Matt had wanted to kiss her. Even though he might wish that it hadn't happened, he couldn't change that. Frankly, she didn't know whether that made her feel better or worse!

They said a stilted goodbye at the front gate. Sharon got into her car and drove home. It was barely ten but she went straight to bed. However, she couldn't sleep. She tossed and turned while her mind replayed what had happened that evening, always coming back to those few, precious minutes in the garden when Matt had kissed her and held her as though he had never wanted to let her go.

It wasn't going to be easy for either of them to forget

what had happened, and her heart ached as she realised how much he must regret it.

'All change, eh? I must admit that I was surprised when Matt announced he was swopping the teams around, but I suppose he must have his reasons. Did he tell you what he was planning, Sharon?'

'No, he never mentioned it.' She summoned a smile as Mike looked curiously at her. 'I'd be the last person he'd discuss his plans with!'

Everyone laughed before the conversation moved on to a new topic. It was a week since the night when Matt had kissed her. Sharon had tried to put it out of her mind and concentrate on her work but it hadn't been easy. Matt had been particularly cool with her since then, so much so that the others had noticed and remarked on it. Now she couldn't help wondering if his decision to reorganise the teams had anything to do with what had happened between them.

From the end of the following month, she and Bert would be working together while Matt would be working with Beth Maguire's team. It would be the perfect way to avoid him having to come into daily contact with her, wouldn't it?

Sharon left the staffroom, knowing that she wouldn't rest until she found out what was going on. Matt was in the office and she tapped on the door. She didn't want to promote an argument but maybe it was time to clear the air. If Matt was making changes to the schedules because of what had happened between them then something needed to be said.

'What can I do for you, Sharon?' He tossed his pen onto the desk when she entered the room. There was a mountain of papers on it so she got straight to the point rather than wasting time.

'I want to know if you've reorganised the rotas because of what happened the other night,' she said flatly.

He didn't pretend not to understand. 'No, it had nothing whatsoever to do with that, I can assure you.'

'Oh.' She felt a bit deflated by his answer and uncomfortable because she wasn't sure what to say next. Matt sighed when he saw her dilemma.

'Look, Sharon, I know we agreed to forget about what happened but obviously it isn't that easy. However, I can assure you that the new rotas have nothing whatsoever to do with you.' He pointed to the heap of papers. 'This is to blame.'

She frowned. 'What do you mean?'

'That there are plans for us to get a second helicopter. It would be marvellous if we could get the funding for it because there's no doubt that it's desperately needed. I'm working on the costings at the moment for Sir Humphrey so that he can present them to the area health authority.

'At present we're funded through a charitable trust but if the area health authority decides to back us then it will make a huge difference. Having two helicopters and crews available twenty-four hours a day will save many more lives.'

'I see, and I agree that there's definitely a need for another air ambulance. But I don't understand why you had to alter the rotas.'

'Because I need to make a full assessment of our staffing requirements. Should we employ a second doctor, for instance?' He shrugged. 'There's no doubt that in some instances it can be useful to have a trained doctor on call to respond to an emergency, although I'm not decrying in any way what you paramedics do when I say that. You are the experts when it comes to front line emergency medical care but there are situations which only a doctor can deal with.

However, it's a question of weighing the extra costs against the benefits.'

'So basically you want to assess the strengths of the teams—is that what you're saying?'

'That's it exactly. Before you joined us there was no chance of me flying with Beth's team. Your predecessor took a lot of time off sick so I needed to make sure we were covered on this shift. But now we have a bit of leeway it means that I can get an overall picture of the service we're offering.'

'I see.' She grimaced. 'Sorry. I seem to have jumped the gun a bit, haven't I? You've been so cool with me lately that I thought it must have something to do what happened, you see.'

'Have I been cool with you, Sharon?'

She heard the troubled note in his voice and sighed. 'Yes. Didn't you realise?'

'No, I didn't.' He pushed back his chair and got up. Walking to the window, he stared across the car park. 'I was trying to treat you exactly the same as everyone else but obviously I got it wrong. I suppose it's only natural in the circumstances.'

'Why do you say that?' she asked quietly, praying that he wouldn't tell her how much he regretted what had gone on.

'Because it isn't easy to think of you in the same way as I think of Bert, for instance,' he explained dryly, glancing at her.

She laughed, relieved that he could joke about the situation. 'Mmm, I can understand that.'

'Can you? Then maybe you can understand why I've gone a bit too far the other way and ended up by being too distant. It wasn't my intention, Sharon, and I apologise for it.'

It was obvious that he was telling the truth and she bit

back a sigh. Even though Matt regretted having treated her so coldly it didn't change anything. He seemed determined to forget what had happened and that hurt, probably more than it should. It had been a kiss, not a promise of undying devotion, for heaven's sake! Yet in the scale of events that had happened in her life it seemed to have taken pole position.

It was a relief when the alarm sounded because it meant that she didn't have time to work out why that kiss had become so important to her. She and Matt hurried from the office and found Mike handing over the incident report to Andy.

'What have we got?' Matt asked as he went over to them.

'Rock-climber fallen in the Yorkshire wolds,' the pilot explained. 'His friend managed to raise the alarm but the fellow is trapped on a ledge so no one knows how badly injured he is. Apparently he's unconscious, but that's all the information we have at the moment.'

'Right, we'd better get going. How long will it take us to get there?' Matt demanded.

'A good thirty minutes at a guess, but I'll have a better idea once I check the co-ordinates,' Andy informed him.

'Here you go.' Mike passed him a slip of paper with the map reference written on it. 'It's not a hundred per cent accurate, I'm afraid. The chap who phoned in the report could only give a rough idea where his friend had fallen. Mountain Rescue are out looking for him at the moment and they'll pass on any info as and when.'

'Oh, great! Like looking for the proverbial needle,' Andy declared pithily.

Sharon grinned. 'Rather a big haystack, too, isn't it? Let's hope the fellow is wearing something nice and bright so we can spot him.'

'Well, you might just have a bit of a problem there.'

Mike grimaced when they all looked at him. 'Sorry, guys, but the forecast is for heavy mist in that area.'

'Seems we'll be looking for that needle whilst wearing blindfolds,' Andy retorted. 'If you've any more good news like that then save it, Henderson. I don't think we want to hear it!'

They all laughed, Mike included, before they hurried off to their respective posts. Sharon couldn't help thinking how good it was to work with such a great team. Most medical professionals shared the same kind of offbeat humour. It was the result of doing a job that constantly taxed the emotions. Dealing with life-and-death situations was never easy so they tended to joke about it because otherwise the work would have become intolerable. It was a kind of safety valve.

It made her wonder once again how Matt coped before she put it from her mind. He dealt with his wife's death in his own way and didn't ask for anyone's sympathy. It was pointless wishing that she could do more when it was obvious that he would resent her interfering.

It took almost forty minutes to reach the area where the climber had been reported missing. As Mike had warned them, the mist was quite thick in patches, making it difficult to spot him. They circled the area half a dozen times before Matt suddenly got a sighting.

'There, roughly three o'clock!'

Sharon twisted round so that she could see out of the window behind her. The mist suddenly parted and she caught a glimpse of a bright yellow jacket on a ledge half-way down the hillside.

'I don't think I'm going to be able to land,' Andy said, studying the rocky terrain. 'I'll get as close as I dare and then you can drop down onto the ledge beside him.'

'Fine,' Matt agreed immediately, looking anxiously out of the window as the helicopter began its descent.

Sharon held her breath as they inched their way towards the injured man. The mountain towered above them and she was very aware of how dangerous it was as the pilot took them as close in as he dared. One small slip and the rotors would clip the rock, which would be disastrous.

'I'm going down first to assess how bad he is,' Matt informed them, opening the door. 'We'll decide what to do after that.'

Sharon knew that he meant they would reassess the situation once they found out if the climber was alive. She watched anxiously as he dropped onto the ledge and inched his way over to the injured man. He looked up, forming his thumb and forefinger into a circle to show that the man was still alive.

Bert dropped a neck brace down to him, then passed him a spinal board. Matt stowed them on the ledge then cupped his hands to his mouth.

'Sharon, can you come down here with me? You're smaller than Bert and there isn't much room to manoeuvre.'

She quickly swung her legs out of the door and let herself drop onto the ledge. Matt steadied her then waved to Andy to tell him that he could pull back while they got the injured man ready to be transferred to the helicopter.

Sharon sighed as the machine moved away. 'That's better. I can hear myself think now.'

Matt grinned as he lined up the spinal board next to the man. 'You wouldn't be saying that if Andy decided to fly off and leave us here.'

'I certainly wouldn't.' She glanced at the mist-shrouded mountains and shivered. 'What on earth possesses people to come climbing in the first place? It's beyond me.'

'It's the challenge, the buzz you get when you realise that you've pitted your strength and wits against nature and won.' He must have seen her surprise because he smiled. 'I used to climb when I was at med school.'

'Really? I would never have put you down as a devotee of dangerous sports,' she exclaimed.

'Because you've heard me expounding about how silly it is to take risks?' He shrugged when she nodded. 'I've taken my fair share of them in my time, but that was before I had Jessica to consider.'

He didn't add anything else but he didn't need to because she understood. Knowing that he had sole responsibility for his daughter, it meant that he had needed to make a number of changes to his life. It struck her once more how much he had given up, although she doubted whether he saw it that way.

Matt wanted to do all he could for Jessica but it was the thought that it was prompted by both guilt and love that worried her. It didn't seem right that he should suffer the added burden of feeling responsible for what had happened when it hadn't been his fault.

They quickly got the injured climber ready to be moved, fitting a cervical collar first before transferring him to the spinal board. Matt had discovered that the man's pelvis was fractured so he had strapped up the lower part of his body to help minimise the risk of any internal damage. They would set up a drip as soon as they got him on board but it was far too complicated to deal with that at the present time.

It took a lot of sheer physical effort plus some superb flying to get the climber safely into the helicopter. Andy pretended to wipe sweat from his brow once they were finally *en route* to the nearest hospital.

'That was hairy! Let's hope the rest of the day is nice and peaceful. I could certainly do with a breather after that!'

'You did a great job,' Matt told him sincerely. 'We could never have got him out of there if it hadn't been for you.'

'Just doing my job, boss,' the pilot demurred.

Sharon laughed. 'There's doing a job and *doing* a job! Don't be so modest.' Her tone was warm because she meant every word. However, she couldn't help noticing the sharp look Matt gave her.

She turned away to check the patient's drip, feeling her heart racing. Matt wasn't jealous! She must get that idea right out of her head. But it was harder than it should have been to dismiss it.

The thought plagued her on the flight to the hospital. The climber regained consciousness on the way, although he was a little confused about what had happened. Matt calmly explained what had gone on and reassured him that his friend was fine.

Sharon couldn't help noticing how quickly he managed to calm the injured man. Matt possessed an air of authority that must have been deeply reassuring to anyone who was injured. He was a caring and commited doctor to his patients and a wonderful father to his daughter. If only he would be easier on himself, and admit that he had needs which neither his role as a physician or a parent could fulfil.

She sighed. Maybe that was expecting too much. Matt was still grieving for his wife and until he had got over her death he could never move on. It made her see how stupid it had been to imagine that he'd been jealous.

They had another call almost as soon as they returned to base. Fortunately, it was relatively straightforward, an almost routine call to a road accident. They flew the injured motorist to hospital then returned to base, and the rest of the day passed without incident.

Mike invited her for a drink after work but Sharon refused. Maybe it was silly to feel self-conscious but she couldn't help wondering what Matt would think if he found out. She went straight home and spent a restless couple of hours prowling the bungalow. There was nothing on television that interested her and she didn't feel like reading.

In the end she decided to go for a walk because it was better than staying in the house by herself.

It brought it home to her that she needed to rebuild her social life. She made up her mind to get in touch with her friends and arrange to meet them. She couldn't spend the rest of her life sitting home alone!

There was a park near to where she lived so she headed in that direction. It was a warm night and there were quite a lot of people in the park, taking advantage of the good weather. Most were couples, strolling along arm in arm or holding hands.

Sharon felt a bit conspicuous on her own so she quickened her pace and headed for the duck pond in the centre of the park. There were always lots of families there on summer evenings, feeding the ducks. She wouldn't stand out so much there or feel so lonely.

'Sharon! Sha-ron!'

She turned when she heard someone calling her and saw Jessica waving to her. She waved back then let her eyes lift to the man who was pushing the wheelchair while she felt her heart surge. In that moment she knew that she would never feel lonely again if she had someone like Matt and his daughter to love and care for.

Was that what was missing from her life—a husband and child? Or was it *this* man she wanted, *his* child she longed to take care of?

She wasn't sure what the answers were and didn't try to work them out. Matt had made it abundantly clear that there was no place for her in his life so there was no point pinning her hopes on an impossible dream.

'I thought you were *never* going to hear me! I was calling and calling your name, wasn't I, Daddy?'

Sharon summoned a smile as Jessica and Matt reached her. 'I'm sorry. I must have been wool-gathering.'

Jessica giggled. 'What a funny thing to say!'

She laughed. 'I suppose it is. It's something my father used to say. He was forever accusing me of wool-gathering because I used to spend so much of my time daydreaming, you see.'

'I do that, too! Daddy calls me Dozy Dilly, the day-dreamer,' Jessica exclaimed.

'And it's the perfect name, too.' Matt said laconically. 'This little madam is in a world of her own most days. Unless it's a cunning ploy to get out of doing her share of the jobs. Mmm, I wonder why I never thought of that before?'

'I did the dishes tonight!' Jessica retorted indignantly. 'I washed *and* dried them.'

Sharon smiled as she listened to the exchange between father and daughter. It was obvious what a good relationship the pair had. Matt was doing a wonderful job of raising his child. He didn't make the mistake of smothering Jessica with attention, but made her do things for herself. Any child would be lucky to have him as a father. Unbidden, the image of a small child with her russet red hair and Matt's thickly lashed green eyes sprang to mind, and she gasped.

'Are you OK?'

She blushed when she found Matt looking at her. The thought that he might be able to read her mind gave her hot and cold chills. 'I'm fine.'

She didn't give him time to question her further as she turned to Jessica. 'So, what are you two doing here? I would have thought you'd be in bed by this time of the night.'

'I don't have to go to school tomorrow,' the little girl informed her. 'We broke up for our summer holidays so I have six whole weeks off!'

'Lucky you!' Sharon smiled at the child's obvious delight. However, although Jessica might be thrilled by the prospect of a long holiday from school, it must present a few problems. She looked questioningly at Matt. 'How are you going to manage while you're at work? Is your sitter going to mind Jessica for you?'

'My parents are coming to stay. They moved to Spain a couple of years ago because the weather there is so much better. But they find it too hot there in the summer so they rent out their villa and spend a couple of months with us instead.'

'How lovely! And it must make life easier, knowing that they're around to look after Jessica during the long summer break,' she said.

'Gramps and Granny said that I can go and stay with them at half term,' Jessica piped up. 'They have a swimming pool at their villa and Gramps said that he would teach me to swim.'

'Nothing has been decided yet, Jess,' Matt said firmly, 'so don't go raising your hopes.'

Sharon didn't say anything but she saw the child's face fall. She found herself wondering if Matt's reluctance to let his daughter stay with her grandparents was because he saw it as offloading his responsibilities. To her mind it was silly to think like that in view of how much he did for the child. However, she knew that it wasn't her place to comment.

Fortunately Jessica soon cheered up. Holding up a crumpled paper bag, she pointed towards the lake. 'Are we going to feed the ducks now, Daddy?'

'Of course.' Matt turned the wheelchair around then paused. 'It was nice to see you, Sharon—' he began, before Jessica interrupted.

'Aren't you coming with us, Sharon? I've got heaps of bread. Look!' She opened the bag so that Sharon could see the thick slices of bread it contained then looked appealingly at her father. 'Ask Sharon to come with us, Daddy—please!'

Matt grimaced. 'You're very welcome to come, of

course. But, please, don't think that you have to. Throwing bread to the ducks isn't exactly *sophisticated* entertainment!'

She laughed when he rolled his eyes. 'Depends what you do for the rest of the time. My social life is hardly one long round of cocktail parties, so feeding the ducks sounds like a very attractive option. It certainly beats sitting on your own in front of the television.'

He shook his head but his smile was gentle. 'You'll have me weeping soon! And I'm sure your social life will soon pick up once everyone knows that you're back in circulation. However, in the absence of any better offers at this precise moment, please, do join us. I find feeding the ducks very therapeutic. It's certainly less stressful than having to make conversation at all those cocktail parties you're going to find yourself attending in years to come!'

Sharon chuckled. 'Why do I get the feeling that was spoken from the heart?'

'It was.' Matt pushed the wheelchair to the lake and set the brake as Jessica began tossing bread into the water. 'I attended umpteen dos like that when I was working at the Royal, usually fund-raising events. It's one aspect of the job I certainly don't miss. There's nothing worse than having to sip a glass of sweet sherry, eat a flaky pastry vol-au-vent *and* make witty conversation with some stranger. Torture—pure, undiluted torture!'

'Don't!' Sharon was laughing so hard that her eyes had started to water. 'Where *do* they find that sherry? It's always the same, isn't it? Oh, it comes in bottles with different labels, but it tastes the same. Do you think it's bottled specially for NHS parties?'

'I'm convinced of it,' he declared. 'There's probably a vineyard somewhere in Spain where the vines are labelled, ''For NHS consumption only.'' Mind you, nobody else would touch it.'

He laughed as well, his green eyes dancing with amusement as they met hers. Sharon felt her breath catch as she looked into his smiling face and saw a glimpse of the carefree man he had been once upon a time.

That Matthew Dempster had been able to laugh at the ridiculous things in life and treat the rest with the gravity they deserved. He had balanced the demands of his work against his own needs, and taken equal pleasure from both. He'd had love in his life, a job he enjoyed and a future to look forward to, but all that had been taken from him the day of the accident.

How she longed to make him see that he could be happy again. If she could show him that he still had a future to look forward to, then...

What?

What did she hope to achieve? Did she imagine that Matt would fall in love with her and they would live happily ever after like two characters in a fairy story?

Sharon felt the shock to the soles of her feet. Of course that wasn't what she wanted to happen. The idea was ridiculous!

She found her eyes lingering on him as he bent to pick up a piece of bread which Jessica had dropped, and felt her heart begin to race.

Wasn't it?

CHAPTER SIX

'ALL gone!'

Jessica emptied the crumbs from the bag then sighed as she watched the ducks milling about on the water. 'I think they're still hungry, Daddy. We should have brought more bread.'

'If they have any more they won't be able to swim! Look, that one can hardly stay afloat because he's so full of bread.' Matt pointed to a handsome, green-headed mallard as Jessica giggled.

'You are silly, Daddy!'

'And you are a cheeky monkey who should be in bed!' He bent and buzzed the child's cheek with his chin, grinning when she squealed. 'Sorry, am I all prickly? I must need a shave.'

Sharon's eyes traced the firm line of his jaw and she felt a tingle race through her. The shadow of beard gave Matt an unaccustomedly rakish air, heightened by the fact that his hair had been mussed by the breeze. He was always impeccably groomed at work so that it was unusual to see him looking like this. She couldn't deny that her senses were stirred by the change in his appearance.

'Have I got a smut on my face or something?' He rubbed his hand over his face when he caught her looking at him.

'No, of course not. I'm sorry if I was staring. I…I was miles away,' she said quickly. It had been a struggle to rid her mind of the fanciful thoughts that had plagued it earlier, and she certainly didn't want to undo all her hard work.

She took a deep breath as he pushed Jessica's chair away from the lake. The park had emptied rapidly in the past half hour and there were few people about as they made their way back up the path. Matt paused when they came to where the path divided, frowning as he saw how dark it looked along the section Sharon needed to take to get home.

'I don't like the thought of you walking home on your own from here, Sharon. How far is it to your house?'

'Oh, not far,' she assured him quickly, not wanting him to worry about her. 'I'll be fine.'

He shot another look along the shadowy path then shook his head. 'We'll see you home. I won't have a minute's peace, wondering if you've got back safely.'

'Are we going to Sharon's house, Daddy?' Jessica demanded. She clapped her hands in delight when he nodded. 'Oh, that's brill! I can't wait to see where you live, Sharon. I told *everyone* at school about you!'

Sharon was touched by the child's enthusiasm. She glanced at Matt and was surprised by the grim expression on his face. He didn't say anything, however, so she decided that it might be best not to ask him what was wrong.

It didn't take long to reach the small bungalow where she lived. Jessica had kept up a lively conversation all the way there, although Sharon was conscious that Matt had said very little. It was obvious that something was troubling him but she had no idea what it was.

When the little girl asked if she could see inside the house, Sharon wasn't sure whether she should agree. In the end, she decided that there was no way she was going to refuse the request just because it might not meet with Matt's approval. If he didn't like the idea then he would have to come out and say so. It wasn't up to her to try and second-guess how he felt!

'Of course you can come in, sweetheart,' she assured her, avoiding Matt's eyes as she opened the front door. 'Would you like a drink and some cake? I baked a sponge cake at the weekend and there's still some left.'

'Yes, please!' Jessica agreed enthusiastically.

Sharon held the door wide open so that Matt could get the wheelchair inside, but once they were in the hallway Jessica was able to manage on her own. She whizzed from room to room, exclaiming excitedly about everything she saw.

'It's brilliant,' she finally declared. 'I can get into the sitting room and the kitchen and the bathroom *and* the bedroom without having to go up any stairs!'

Sharon laughed. 'That's right. My father couldn't get up and down stairs after he was taken ill, you see, so that's why we moved here. Still, you have a lift at home so you're able to use that to get upstairs, aren't you?'

'Uh-huh, but not by myself 'cos I can't get into the seat on my own. Someone has to help me,' Jessica explained without a shred of self-pity. 'This is better because I wouldn't need anyone to help me if I lived here. I could be just like everyone else then, couldn't I?'

Sharon wasn't sure what to reply because she didn't want to say something out of turn. She glanced at Matt for guidance and saw that he was frowning. Obviously, the comment had come as something of a surprise to him.

'How about that drink?' she suggested, diplomatically changing the subject. 'What would you like? Milk or juice?'

She led the way to the kitchen with Jessica bowling along behind her, still talking fifteen to the dozen. Once she had poured her a glass of milk and cut her a slice of the sponge cake, she turned to Matt, who had followed them into the room. 'Coffee?'

'If you're having one, but don't go to any trouble on my account,' he replied evenly.

Jessica quickly finished her snack then asked if she could watch television because there was a programme on that she wanted to see. Sharon agreed at once, smiling as she watched the little girl zoom out of the room.

'She can really get around in that chair, can't she? It's a small consolation that she doesn't seem to let her handicap slow her down.'

'It is, although she does get very frustrated at times when there's something she can't manage by herself.'

Sharon sighed as she switched on the kettle. 'You're thinking about what Jessica said earlier about not being able to use the lift on her own.'

'Yes. I never realised that she found it tiresome to have to wait to be helped.'

'You can't think of everything, Matt,' she said sharply, then shrugged when he looked at her in surprise. 'I get the impression that you are trying to cover every possible problem that Jessica will encounter. It's understandable, but you mustn't feel that you're letting her down because you haven't thought of everything.'

'I expect you're right.' He took a deep breath and his eyes were filled with sadness. 'I just feel that I owe it to her to make her life as *normal* as possible.'

'Because you still feel that you're to blame for what happened?' She shook her head in despair. 'When will you accept that it wasn't your fault? It was an accident and you weren't responsible.'

'One part of me knows that but the other...' He shrugged, not needing to say anything more.

'At some point you're going to have to accept that you can't do everything for Jessica,' she said quietly, picking up the kettle to make the coffee. 'The time will come when she wants to go out into the world by herself and you'll have to let her.'

'Do you think I don't know that?' He sounded annoyed all of a sudden and she looked at him in dismay.

'I'm sure you do. And I didn't mean to poke my nose in where it isn't wanted,' she replied stiffly. 'I'm sorry if that's what you thought I was doing.'

'It's me who should be apologising, Sharon. I didn't mean to bite your head off.' He took the cup from her and sat down. 'And I'm very aware that I can't fulfil all Jessica's needs no matter how hard I try.'

She heard the ache in his voice and knew that he must be thinking about his wife and everything she could have done for the little girl. 'You are doing a wonderful job, Matt. It can't be easy and you are more than rising to the challenge.'

'That doesn't alter the fact that I can't make up for everything Jessica has missed out on by losing her mother, does it?' He looked at the cake that Sharon had left on the table and grimaced. 'I certainly can't bake!'

She laughed, as he'd intended her to, although her heart still ached at the thought of how he constantly tortured himself. Matt was a good father—an *excellent* father!—but he didn't seem to realise that. Few men would have given up so much for their child, although he wouldn't thank her for saying so. She deliberately kept her tone light.

'Not very PC in these days to want to teach your daughter to cook, is it?'

'Probably not, but in the real world where all those politically correct people don't live, little girls like learning things *like* baking and sewing. Of course, little boys probably enjoy them, too, but as I haven't got a son, I can't say for certain. All I know is that my baking and sewing skills fall far short of what is required to teach my daughter!'

'So get someone else to teach her.' It was on the tip of her tongue to offer her services but she was sure that would be met with a refusal. 'How about your mother? She could show Jessica how to bake when she comes to stay with you.'

He burst out laughing. 'You obviously don't know my mother! The PC lobby would embrace her with open arms. Her view has always been that life is too short to spend it in the kitchen. Fortunately, my parents were able to afford a housekeeper otherwise we would have starved!'

'Oh, so I'm talking to one of the privileged of this world, am I? Housekeeper, indeed!' she teased.

'I don't know about privileged. It came as a salutary shock when I went to med school and had to learn how to cook for myself. Oh, I can manage the basics, so we get by just fine, but as for the rest...'

'I could teach Jessica to bake if you like,' she offered, unable to hold back any longer.

'I couldn't let you do that, Sharon. It isn't fair to expect you to waste your time on my daughter.'

'It wouldn't be a waste of my time! I'd be happy to do it. I really like Jessica and I think she likes me.'

'She does. She's never stopped talking about you since we went to the cinema together.'

'But?' She laughed shortly. 'There was a definite *but* tagged on there, Matt.'

'*But* I don't want her getting too attached to you.' He looked up and she could tell at once that he had made up his mind and nothing would change it.

'Jessica has been through enough in her life and there's no way that I'll risk her getting hurt again. I know you mean well, Sharon, and I appreciate it, but I don't want Jessica growing too fond of you. You have your own life to lead and you won't want to spend all your time looking after my daughter.'

She looked down at her coffee because she didn't want

him to see how hurt she felt. Matt might have used Jessica as the excuse to refuse her help, but she wasn't silly enough to think that was all he had meant. He had wanted her to know that there was no place for her in *his* life either.

A small uncomfortable silence fell so that it was a relief when Jessica came back to tell them that her programme had finished. Matt quickly drank his coffee then stood up.

'We'd better be on our way,' he explained politely. 'Thanks for the coffee and everything, Sharon.'

'You're welcome,' she told him equally politely. 'I appreciate you walking me home.'

'It was no trouble.' There was the faintest tinge of impatience in his voice as he continued the game of manners, but she didn't make the mistake of looking for its cause. She saw them to the door, where Jessica insisted on kissing her goodbye. Tears welled into her eyes as she put her arms around the child's thin little body and hugged her, but she quickly blinked them away. Crying wouldn't help. It certainly wouldn't change the situation.

Sharon spent the rest of the evening in front of the television, refusing to let her thoughts stray from the complicated plot of the film that was being shown. She would get on with her life, forget about Matt and his daughter and look to the future, instead of moping.

It all sounded so *easy* in theory but she suspected that putting it into practice was going to be far more difficult. Maybe there was no place for her in Matt's life but he was becoming an increasingly important part of hers.

The next two weeks passed in a blur. Sharon was frantically busy both in and out of work. Determined to stick to her decision to get on with her life, she had phoned her friends and let them know that she was back in circulation. It resulted in a rash of invitations so that she was out every night. She knew that she was burning the candle at both ends but it seemed better than sitting around, brooding.

There was a party on Saturday night, being held by a friend of a friend, so she went along. Several of the party-goers had seen her picture in the paper so she spent a lot of time explaining about her job. One man in particular seemed very interested, although after a while she began to suspect that he was more interested in *her* than the work she did.

She did her best to respond to his overtures but her heart wasn't in it. When he suggested that they have dinner the following week, she politely refused the invitation. Oh, he was pleasant enough but there was no spark there as far as she was concerned. He certainly didn't make her feel how Matt managed to do!

It was unsettling to realise it so she didn't dwell on it. Instead, she told herself that she was having a wonderful time and stayed right to the end of the party to prove it. Consequently, it was her own fault that she had a thumping headache the following day when she went into work.

'Looks like someone had a good night,' Mike observed cheerily when he came into the staffroom and found her slumped in a chair.

'I did, although I'm regretting it now.' She winced when Andy let the door slam behind him. 'Don't do that! My head is fit to bust.'

'What you need is Uncle Andy's tried and tested hang-over remedy,' the pilot declared. 'It's guaranteed to put you back on your feet in no time.'

Sharon didn't bother explaining that it was tiredness that had caused her headache, not alcohol. She rarely drank more than a glass of wine even at parties, preferring to stick to tonic water. However, she doubted whether anyone would believe her so she didn't waste her breath.

'Sounds good to me. How about playing the ministering angel and mixing me up a dose?' she suggested.

'Coming right up!' Andy went to the cupboard and found what he needed. He brought the frothing glass back to her. 'Drink it all up now.'

Sharon studied it warily then shut her eyes and gulped it down in one go. She pulled a face after she'd finished. 'It tasted absolutely disgusting!'

'But it will do you a power of good.' He looked round and grinned as Matt came into the room. 'Looks like we might have another taker for Uncle Andy's remedy. If you don't mind me saying so, you look like one of the walking dead. Dare I ask what you've been up to?' The pilot shot an amused look at Sharon. 'Or is that a leading question?'

Sharon felt the colour flood to her cheeks when she realised what he meant. She didn't dare look at Matt. Would he think that she had given the pilot reason to believe they had spent the previous evening together?

'Put it down to lack of sleep. Nothing more exciting than that, I'm afraid,' Matt explained shortly. He held up the sheet of paper he was carrying, effectively putting a stop to any more questions. 'I just received a fax from the area health authority confirming that they are ready to consider our proposal for an additional air ambulance. I thought you'd all like to know that at least it's being discussed.'

'That's great!' Andy declared, speaking for them all. 'It would make a huge difference if we got the go-ahead.'

'It certainly would,' Matt agreed. 'Beth Maguire was telling me that they had to refuse a call last night because they were already committed to attending a motorway incident. With two helicopters available we wouldn't be placed in that kind of dilemma.'

'What happened?' Sharon asked. She hurried on, trying

to ignore the chill in his eyes as he took stock of her tired face. 'At the incident that they had to turn down, I mean.'

'I've no idea. A ground crew attended instead so it wasn't our problem.' He turned when Mike asked him something else then left the staffroom a few minutes later without speaking to her again. However, Sharon was left with the distinct impression that he wasn't pleased with her.

She sighed as she got up to make a cup of coffee. So what else was new?

It was an unusually quiet day. They had no calls until mid-afternoon when Matt called them into the office. As soon as Sharon saw his face, she knew that it was going to be something out of the ordinary. He got straight to the point.

'We've had an urgent call to an oil rig anchored in the North Sea. They have two men on board suffering from some sort of fever. We have no further information as to what might have caused the problem, just that they are in a pretty bad way.'

'I thought those oil rigs had their own medics on board?' Mike queried. Matt sighed.

'They do, but as luck would have it their own doctor was flown home to Ireland yesterday for a funeral. The oil company has asked if we can attend as the situation is apparently serious.' He glanced at Roy Price, the relief paramedic. 'I know you're covering while Bert is on holiday, but we won't have room for all of us to go if we need to airlift two patients. Sharon and I will deal with this.'

He continued briskly when Roy nodded. 'We do have a problem, I'm afraid. Apparently, there is a bad weather front building over the North Sea. According to the latest forecast, we should have just enough time to get out there, pick up the men and get back home. I'm keeping my fingers crossed that the weather guys have got it right, but we aren't going to have much leeway.'

He didn't add anything, neither did he need to. Everyone knew how dangerous it would be if they were caught in the storm. Nobody said very much as they hurried to board the helicopter. Andy ran through the flight checks in record time then they were airborne and heading out over Humberside. There was a heavy bank of clouds on the horizon and, once they had crossed the coast, Sharon could see the waves churning below them. She found herself uttering a short prayer that they would make it back to land before the storm reached them.

'It will be all right, Sharon. We'll be there and back in no time, you'll see.'

Matt sounded so confident that suddenly she didn't feel scared any longer. With him there beside her then she could face anything.

Her heart ached as she realised how foolish it was to think like that. Matt had his own life to lead and she had hers. There certainly wasn't any future for them together.

'Not landed on anything like this since I left the air force,' Andy observed laconically as they hovered over the oil rig. 'Let's hope I haven't lost the old magic touch, eh?'

Sharon sincerely hoped so! Now that they were over the rig she couldn't help thinking how small it looked in the vastness of the sea. It was hard to believe that there were dozens of men living and working on board the metal construction.

She held her breath as the helicopter began to descend. It couldn't have been easy to bring it in to land when the wind kept buffeting them about. She let out an audible sigh of relief when the helicopter touched down on the landing pad, earning herself a reproachful look from Andy.

'Oh, ye of little faith. Remind me not to ask you for a reference.'

'Sorry!' She grinned apologetically. 'It's not that I don't think you're a superb pilot but this wind is really strong.'

'It is,' Matt said before the pilot could answer. 'Which is why we need to get a move on and not sit here, wasting time.'

He thrust open the door and jumped down onto the deck. Andy gave her a thumbs-up sign but she could tell that he was surprised by Matt's curtness. Sharon sighed as she climbed out of the helicopter. One minute Matt was being considerate, the next he was being curt. Was it any wonder that she felt confused?

'Hi, I'm Frank Cassidy. I'm in charge of the rig. Glad you guys could make it.'

Sharon smiled at the grey-haired man who had come to meet them. 'I would say it's nice to be here only I haven't yet made up my mind about that!'

Frank laughed. 'It does take a bit of getting used to! I'll give you that. Anyway, come on below. That wind is really getting up now so let's not linger out here.'

He quickly led the way to a metal staircase that gave access to the living quarters. Sharon followed him down, with Matt bringing up the rear. Frank led them into what was obviously the office and closed the door.

'Now we can hear ourselves think. First of all I'm really glad that you've come. We've now got three men down with this bug and they're in a pretty bad way, I'm afraid.'

'I'm Dr Matt Dempster, co-ordinator of the East Pennine Air Ambulance Service, and this is Sharon Lennard, one of our paramedics.'

Matt quickly made the introductions. 'When you say that you have three men who are ill, do you mean that they are all exhibiting the same symptoms?'

'More or less. The two who were taken ill yesterday are in a worse state, but I'm ninety-nine per cent certain they are all suffering from the same thing, whatever that is,' Frank explained. 'It would have to happen when Doc Martindale is away, wouldn't it?'

'Par for the course,' Matt agreed sympathetically. 'Right, we'd better take a look at them. If they need airlifting to hospital, which sounds likely, then we'll have to get a move on and do it before the storm breaks. However, I'm afraid that we can only take two at a time, so we may need to come back for the third man later.'

'I understand. Anyway, I'll take you down to the sick bay. I've got one of the guys there playing nurse.' Frank winked at Sharon. 'I imagine even in their sorry state the men will be pleased to see you. Gerry doesn't have the right touch when it comes to playing the ministering angel!'

They all laughed, although Sharon could tell that he was really concerned about his men. He led the way along a series of passageways to the sick bay, which turned out to be a couple of white-painted cabins furnished with regulation hospital beds.

Gerry, the stand-in nurse, was a grizzled man in his late forties with a bushy grey beard and a pair of shoulders a rugby player would have envied. Sharon bit back a grin when they shook hands and she found her fingers enveloped in his massive paw. The gentle touch would be very difficult to achieve with hands that large!

Matt went straight to the first bed and quickly introduced himself. 'I'm Dr Matthew Dempster from the East Pennine Air Ambulance service. Can you tell me when you first felt ill?'

'Day before yesterday I felt a bit crook.' The young man in the bed had a strong Australian accent. He looked to be in his late twenties and despite his tan was very grey and drawn. 'Started off with a hell of a fever—felt as though I was burning up, it did. Then I couldn't stop shivering and my head's been aching something rotten. As if that wasn't bad enough, I've got all these lumps everywhere. Hurt like blazes, they do.'

'I see.' Matt turned to Sharon and she was surprised by the gravity of his expression. 'Can you pass me a pair of gloves, please, Sharon? And put some on yourself.'

She did as he'd said, watching intently while he examined the young man. He paid particular attention to a smooth oval, reddened swelling in his neck. She could see that the skin around it was dark and almost bruised-looking.

'Now, I just need to check your groin and under your arms.' Matt drew back the sheet. Sharon could see there were a number of similar swellings in other parts of the young man's body as well. Frankly, she had never seen anything like them before and had no idea what they were.

Matt covered him up and peeled off his gloves. There was a plastic waste container beside the bed and he carefully deposited them in it then put on a fresh pair of gloves before examining the next man.

Although Sharon had no idea what was wrong with the men, she could tell that Matt was very concerned by what he had found. The atmosphere was extremely tense by the time he had examined the third man and discovered that he had the same symptoms as the others.

'I'm going to start you all on a course of tetracycline,' he informed them, glancing at Sharon, who immediately opened the case they had brought with them. He quickly administered the drugs to each of the men, once again taking great care to dispose of the latex gloves he'd been wearing.

'So what have we got, then, Doc? Come on, you can tell us.'

The Australian summoned a smile but Sharon could tell it was an effort. The other two men hadn't said very much, apart from answering Matt's questions. She suspected that they both felt too ill to talk.

'I'm afraid that everything points to the fact that the three of you have contracted bubonic plague,' he replied flatly.

Sharon gasped. 'Bubonic plague…in this day and age? It doesn't seem possible!'

'I'm afraid it is, though. There are still many parts of the world where bubonic plague poses a real problem.' He looked at the young Australian, who had turned an even ghastlier colour after hearing the news. 'I don't know where you lot caught it but I'm ninety-nine per cent certain that's what you've got.'

''Struth, Doc! You sure know how to hit a guy when he's down. So what happens now? They will be able to treat us at the hospital, won't they?'

'Yes,' Matt said firmly. 'Bubonic plague can be treated very successfully with antibiotics, which is why I've started you on that tetracycline. However, you won't be flown to hospital just yet, I'm afraid. I need to make some arrangements first before we can move you.'

'What sort of arrangements?' Sharon's mouth was so dry that she could barely get the words out. She knew very little about bubonic plague except that it had killed millions of people centuries ago.

'Bubonic plague is a quarantinable disease. It means that I need to notify the hospital that will be caring for these men so that they can take the necessary steps to prepare for them.' Matt paused and she found herself holding her breath as she waited for him to continue.

'It also means that everyone who has come into contact with them will need to be isolated. Basically, nobody can leave here until the correct procedures are put into operation.'

'You mean that *we* have to stay here as well? But for how long?' she demanded, scarcely able to take in what he was saying.

'For however long it takes, I'm afraid. But we certainly won't be leaving before the storm hits. So it will probably be morning before we get away from here.'

Sharon didn't know what to say. It was such a shock. She looked at the others and could see that they were as stunned as she was. She took a deep breath but it didn't help. She was about to spend the night on an oil rig in the middle of a storm.

Her mind made a small sideways leap. Forget the storm. She was about to spend the night on an oil rig with Matt!

CHAPTER SEVEN

'ANDY got back OK. They've called in Beth so she and Roy can take over the rest of our shift. At least we're covered at that end.'

Sharon summoned a smile as Matt came back to tell her what was happening. However, it was hard to drum up much enthusiasm for what was going on back at base. 'That's good.'

Matt sighed. 'I know how you must feel, Sharon, but there isn't anything we can do about it. Until all the correct procedures have been put into place, we're stuck here. We'll just have to make the best of it, I'm afraid.'

'I know. I suppose I'm still a bit shell-shocked,' she told him quickly. In the past hour she had tried to come to terms with what had happened. It hadn't been easy but she was determined to handle this unexpected turn of events in a professional manner. Her personal feelings about being stranded on the rig with Matt weren't the issue.

She glanced around the sick bay as she resolutely confined her thoughts to work. All three patients were fast asleep now and Gerry was sitting in an armchair, reading a lurid-looking paperback novel. Frank had disappeared to contact his bosses and tell them what had happened. It would cause the oil company a massive problem if the whole rig had to be quarantined, but there was nothing anyone could do except comply with health regulations.

'It's no wonder,' Matt observed softly, drawing her towards the door. He waited until they were outside in the corridor before continuing. 'I feel a bit that way myself, to be honest. I could hardly believe my eyes when I saw that bubo—that lump—on Sandy's neck.'

'You were quick to realise what it was. How come you know the signs so well? Bubonic plague isn't your everyday sort of illness when you live in the UK.'

'It certainly isn't, I'm glad to say.' He grimaced. 'I did a stint in India after I'd qualified. It's rife there so I got a good grounding in what to look out for. It was still rather a shock to see it here in the middle of the North Sea, though!'

She laughed at that, although she suspected that he was deliberately trying to lighten the mood for her benefit. 'I can believe it! I wonder where they contracted it.'

'It appears that the three of them have just come back from leave. Frank told me that they'd been visiting Lee's parents in California,' he explained, referring to another of the three men.

'You aren't saying that they caught the disease there?' Sharon exclaimed in disbelief.

'It's possible. There are a number of cases of bubonic plague reported each year in the US. I don't know if you know much about the disease.' He carried on when she shook her head. 'Well, the bacterium responsible for it is found in rodents and usually spreads through flea bites. In other words, a person gets bitten by a flea that has previously bitten a rodent which was carrying the disease.

'It used to be called the Black Death because of the darkening of the skin that occurs. Millions of people died of it during the fourteenth century. It was rats that spread it then but nowadays one of the main culprits for passing on the plague to humans is the domestic cat.'

'Cats? Really?'

'Yes. They pick up the disease from infected fleas or rodents then pass it on when they lick or scratch their owners. Fortunately, it's treatable with modern-day antibiotics and usually isn't life-threatening so long as it's caught early enough. I'm keeping my fingers crossed that we've caught this outbreak in time.'

'Oh, I hope so. It doesn't bear thinking about if we haven't.' She gave an involuntary shudder and heard him sigh.

'Which is why we aren't going to dwell on it. We're going to be positive about this. Understand?'

'Yes, Dr Dempster, sir,' she replied pertly, with a smile that seemed to freeze on her lips when she saw the way he was looking at her. There was a moment when she sensed that he was going to say something then Frank arrived and it passed.

'Right, I've been on to headquarters and they are less than pleased, I can tell you. My boss has been in touch with the Chief Medical Officer's department and they have laid down the law about what we can and cannot do.'

'Good. They need to take a firm hand in a situation like this,' Matt stated emphatically. 'The last thing anyone wants is for this to spread.'

'That's basically what they've told my boss.' Frank shrugged. 'Anyway, the outcome of it all is that the company is sending out a team of doctors and nurses tomorrow. Everyone on board the rig is to be treated with antibiotics as a precaution. All leave has been cancelled and the medics will stay here for the next two weeks so that they are on hand in case anyone else comes down with it. How likely is it that we'll have any more cases, Doc?'

'Not very. The most infectious form of plague is pneumonic plague, which affects the lungs. It's often a complication of bubonic plague and is highly contagious because it's spread through airborne droplets being expelled during coughing. However, none of the men are showing any signs of it, I'm happy to say.'

'Well, that's one blessing at least.' Frank shook his head.

'I still can't believe this has happened but I suppose we just have to get on and deal with it. By the way, the helicopter that is bringing out the medics tomorrow will fly you all to hospital. My boss has been in contact with your base and he was told that they can't risk having your helicopter contaminated.'

'That's right. We would need to fumigate the helicopter if we used it and that would cause problems. We can't afford to have it out of commission for any length of time. You do realise that all the bedding and everything else that the men have been using will need to be disposed of?' Matt warned him.

'So I believe. I shall have to add housekeeping duties to my job description. Oh, and on that subject, I've found you a cabin for tonight. I'm afraid you two will have to bunk up together because we've only got the one spare. I'll show you where it is.'

Frank led the way down the corridor but it was a moment before Sharon followed him. She didn't look at Matt because she didn't dare. Think like a *professional*, she told herself sternly, but it didn't do a lot to quieten her racing heart.

'Here you are. It isn't the Ritz, but you'll find everything you need.'

Frank opened the cabin door so they could see inside. Sharon took quick stock of the twin bunk beds and the shower stall set into one corner of the room, and gulped. It was a blessing that Frank didn't seem to require her to say anything.

'We eat early so dinner's at six. Just come along when you're ready and I'll see you there.' He sketched them a wave then hurried off.

Sharon counted to ten—slowly—then glanced at Matt. He wasn't looking at her, however. He was staring into the cabin with an expression on his face that made her long to know what he was thinking, before it struck her what a mistake that could be.

Stick to professional, Sharon! she told herself, repeating the mantra as though her life depended on it. Maybe it did. Maybe her whole future hinged on her remembering that Matt wasn't interested in anything apart from his job and his daughter.

'I'm going to put through a call to Jessica to let her know what's happened. I don't want her worrying.'

She summoned a smile when he turned. 'Fine. It's a good job your parents are here, isn't it?'

'Yes, it would have been very awkward otherwise,' he agreed evenly. He shot another look around the cabin then shrugged. 'Look, Sharon, I'm not bothered about having a place to sleep tonight. I'll stay in the sick bay so that I can keep an eye on the men. You can have the cabin to yourself.'

'Fine by me,' she agreed airily. 'I think I'll take a shower if you don't need me. I'll see you at dinner.'

She went inside the cabin and closed the door while he went on his way. She caught a glimpse of herself in the mirror next to the shower and grimaced. So much for worrying if she would be able to behave like a professional. Matt obviously had no intention of putting either of them to the test!

There was a crowd of men gathered in the dining room when Sharon arrived that evening. It was obvious that news of her presence on board the rig had spread like wildfire because every head swivelled in her direction. She paused uncertainly by the door, embarrassed by the amount of attention she was attracting. It was a relief when Matt suddenly appeared at her side.

'We're over there, sitting with Frank. I was just going to

the buffet to see what I fancied so we may as well go together.'

'Thanks.' She gave him a grateful smile. 'I feel just a *tiny* bit conspicuous!'

He laughed. 'I can understand why. Still, you can't blame these guys for staring. It isn't every day of the week that a beautiful woman turns up in their midst. They probably think that Christmas has come early this year!'

She laughed out loud. 'Thanks...I think!'

She followed him to the counter and picked up a tray. There was a good choice on the menu so it wasn't difficult to find something that appealed to her. A chicken breast in a delicious mushroom sauce and freshly prepared vegetables soon found themselves onto her tray. She added a bottle of mineral water and the requisite cutlery then followed Matt to their table.

Frank grinned as she sat down. 'Sorry about the guys staring like that. It never fails to amaze me how fast word gets round this place when something out of the ordinary happens.' He looked pointedly around the crowded canteen. 'Last time I saw it this busy in here was when we were showing a rerun of England playing in the World Cup!'

Sharon couldn't help laughing. 'Then I'm truly flattered. To rank alongside something really important like football is indeed an honour!'

Matt grinned as he pulled out a chair and sat down. 'Not just any old game of football, mind, but the *World Cup*. You *should* be flattered!'

She smiled back at him, thinking how relaxed he looked that night. He must have found time to shower because his hair was still damp, curling slightly where it touched his collar at the back. Like her, he had shed his flight suit and was wearing jeans and a blue check cotton shirt. He had rolled up his sleeves and left the collar unbuttoned and she couldn't help thinking how different he looked that night, so much more at ease.

How much time had he spent away from Jessica since the accident? she wondered. She doubted if there had been many occasions when he had delegated his responsibilities, and she was suddenly glad that he had this night to himself, even if it was in the most peculiar of circumstances.

Conversation flowed easily throughout the meal. Frank introduced them to the other people at their table and they spent a pleasant couple of hours chatting about incidentals. After her initial self-consciousness, Sharon soon found herself relaxing. Although she had created a stir in the all-male community, none of the men said anything to make her feel uncomfortable. Most of them were happily married and she spent a lot of time admiring photos of various wives and children.

'Well, this has been very pleasant but I'd better go and take a look at my patients.' Matt pushed back his chair. He glanced at her when she rose as well. 'You don't need to come, Sharon.'

'I'd like to see how they are. And I thought I'd give Gerry a bit of a breather,' she explained.

'That should cheer the guys up,' Frank observed laconically. 'Gerry's heart's in the right place but let's just say that it's a damn good job he decided to go into oil drilling rather than nursing.'

Everyone laughed, Sharon included. She followed Matt from the dining room, glad that he seemed to know the way to the sick bay.

'I don't know how you remember which way to go,' she declared, following him along the maze of corridors.

'Oh, the old Scout training comes up trumps every time,' he proclaimed, grinning at her. They turned a corner and ground to a halt when they were confronted with a blank wall.

Sharon chuckled. 'You were saying?'

'OK, so *occasionally* I get it wrong. I never said I was infallible, did I?'

'No. Covered yourself there, didn't you, Dr Dempster?' she teased. 'Nobody could ever accuse you of making false claims.'

'Certainly not. I'm far too wily for that!'

He treated her to a smile that made her pulse race. Placing his hands on her shoulders, he briskly turned her round and steered her back the way they had come. 'I think it should have been left not right here,' he explained when they came to a fork in the corridor.

Sharon lifted a slender brow. 'Are you sure?'

'Positive!' He folded his arms across his chest and pretended to glare at her. 'I hope you don't have any doubts that I know what I'm doing, Miss Lennard. That smacks of rank insubordination to me.'

'Oh, have mercy, Captain! Please, don't have me keel-hauled, I beg you,' she pleaded, hamming it up.

'That could be a little difficult on an oil rig,' he replied tartly, shaking his head. 'You are one crazy lady, do you know that?'

'Am I?' She laughed when he pulled a face. 'Don't answer that! OK, Captain, which way now?'

'Down here, I think.' Matt started down the other section of corridor but it soon became obvious that they were hopelessly lost. Sharon tried her hardest not to laugh but his expression was so comical that she couldn't help it.

'Come on, admit it—you haven't a clue where we are!' she taunted.

'Rubbish! I just thought that you would appreciate a guided tour of the rig.' He pointed to a door on their left. 'That's one of the cabins and this...' he pointed to a door on their right '...is another cabin. See? I know exactly where we are.'

'Oh, I can see that all right. I don't know why I ever doubted you,' she declared, laughing so hard that her sides ached.

Matt treated her to a baleful stare. 'Why do I get the feeling that you're sending me up, Miss Lennard?'

'Would I do that?' she spluttered, wiping her streaming eyes with the back of her hand.

'Yes, you certainly would.' His face broke into a huge smile. 'Nobody could stand on his dignity for long with you around, that's for sure.'

'Good. It's good to laugh at yourself once in a while. You can't always take life so seriously.'

'Sometimes it's hard to find much to laugh about.'

She sighed when she heard the suddenly flat note in his voice. 'I know but life is for living, Matt. It's a sin to let it pass you by.'

'Thanks for the advice.' He started to move on but she stopped him by dint of a well-placed hand on his arm.

'But you aren't going to heed it?' There was a touch of asperity in her voice that brought his eyes to her face. Sharon saw the chill that had invaded them again and wished with all her heart that she hadn't said that and ruined the light-hearted mood. However, there was no way that she could back down now. 'You're determined not to have a life of your own, aren't you?'

'I don't want to discuss this—' he began, but she didn't let him finish.

'I know you don't! The same as I know that it hasn't anything to do with me! But I can't help saying something, Matt. I know how much you love Jessica and I understand why you want to do everything you can for her. But it's wrong to forget about your own needs in the process.'

'What needs? If you mean sex then why not come right out and say so?' His eyes blazed into hers and she took an instinctive step back. 'I've not slept with a woman since

Claire died, so what does that say about my needs, I wonder? Come on, Sharon, you're the one with all the answers, so you tell me.'

She didn't know what to say. Maybe it was the anger in his voice which had stolen her ability to speak, or maybe it was the shock of hearing that he had been celibate since his wife had died, but she couldn't think of a single word to say to him.

He uttered something harsh as he brushed past her. Sharon didn't attempt to follow him. Somehow she found her way to her cabin and lay on the bunk. It felt as though her heart were being slowly crushed because she knew that Matt would never forgive her for what she had done.

How he must hate her for making him reveal something so personal.

She must have fallen asleep because she awoke with a start when someone knocked on the cabin door. Fumbling her way across the room in the dark, she opened the door and felt her heart sink when she found Matt outside.

'I'm sorry. I didn't mean to disturb you,' he said shortly. 'Frank said to tell you that they're showing a film you might like to see, but it doesn't matter.' He turned to leave but she couldn't let him go without at least attempting to apologise for what she had said earlier.

'No, wait. I...I'd like to see it.' She took a deep breath. 'But there's something I want to say to you first, so will you come in?' She quickly switched on the light and stepped back, but he made no attempt to enter the cabin.

'Look, Sharon, it isn't—'

'I think I owe—'

They both spoke together then stopped. Matt shrugged as he stepped inside the cabin. 'You go first.'

'I just want to apologise for what I said earlier.' She stared at the floor because she was afraid that her courage would desert her if she looked at him. 'I was out of order, Matt. I had no right to say what I did.'

'I had no right to snap at you like that either, so I guess that makes us quits.' He gave a soft laugh but she heard the uncertainty it held. It brought her eyes winging to his face and she frowned. He didn't look angry, funnily enough, only sad, and she couldn't help wondering why.

'It's good of you to see it that way.' She gave a small, rather helpless shrug, knowing that she owed it to him to be truthful. 'I don't know what got into me, to be honest. It isn't like me to say something like that.'

'You said what you thought was true.'

'Yes, I did. But it wasn't my place to say it, was it?' She looked away, feeling the sting in the tail of that comment. She didn't have any right to pass judgement on how he lived his life, and it hurt to have to face up to it.

'I think you said it because you care, Sharon. I appreciate that.'

'Do you?' She couldn't look at him when she heard the beseeching note in her voice. If only she could treat this situation dispassionately, it would be so much easier. However, it was hard to be objective, as she desperately wanted to be.

'Yes, I do.' He took a deep breath then let it out in a sigh that echoed with sadness. 'It's good to know that you care about me even though it doesn't change the situation.'

There was such finality in his voice that her eyes stung with tears. 'Why, Matt? Why are you so determined to stick to the status quo?' she implored him. 'Is it because you want to punish yourself for what happened?'

She held her breath, wondering if once again she had gone too far and asked a question she shouldn't have asked.

'I can't help feeling guilty, Sharon. I keep thinking how different things might have been if I hadn't been late that day.' He shook his head when she went to speak but there was no impatience on his face, just a sadness that made her want to weep for what he was going through.

'No, I know what you're going to say. I've heard it all before, but until I can believe it here, in my heart, I can't accept it. However, it isn't just guilt that holds me back from looking for another relationship. I'm just not prepared to risk being hurt again, basically. I would rather spend the rest of my life on my own than go through what I went through when Claire died.'

Sharon couldn't hold back her tears any longer when she heard him say that. It made her realise how foolish it was to hope that he might ever change his mind.

'Don't! Please, don't cry. I hate to see you upset like this.' He enfolded her in his arms and held her as he would have held Jessica if she'd been upset. It just served to make her cry all the harder when she realised it, and she heard him sigh.

'Sharon, I'm not worth all these tears. You have your own life to lead and you mustn't worry about me. I'll be fine…perfectly fine.'

'How can you be fine?' she gulped, her voice thickened with tears. 'You're deliberately denying yourself any chance of happiness. It's wrong, Matt. Wrong!'

She looked up at him with swimming eyes, willing him to understand that he was making a mistake.

He shook his head, a slight smile curving his lips. 'You don't give up easily, do you?'

'No. When I think something is wrong, I do everything I can to change it.'

'I'm almost tempted to believe that you could make it happen, too,' he said softly. He brushed back her hair then let his fingers follow the contours of her cheek. Sharon shivered when she felt his fingertips gliding over her skin. There was an oddly pensive look on his face as he let them skim up to her temple.

She held her breath, not daring to breathe in case she broke the spell. She had a feeling that he wasn't fully aware of what he was doing as he let his fingers slide into her hair.

'You have beautiful hair, Sharon,' he murmured. 'It's so thick and silky.'

He slid a russet curl through his fingers and she shivered, not proof against how it made her feel to have him touch her like that. However, when she felt his hand slide to the nape of her neck she couldn't hold back the murmur that sprang from her lips and she felt him tense. For a moment his eyes blazed into hers and she was shaken by the depth of emotion she saw in them before he abruptly released her.

'Now it's my turn to apologise. I shouldn't have done that.' His tone was clipped but she knew that was because he was as shaken as she was by what had happened.

It was like a small glimmer of light at the end of a very dark tunnel, and she stored it away. Maybe—just *maybe*—Matt wasn't a totally lost cause after all?

'Which film are they showing tonight?' she asked, deliberately changing the subject. She wouldn't overcome all Matt's objections in one fell swoop so she would need to be patient.

She frowned, wondering why it was so important that she should convince him that he had a future to look forward to.

'That new romantic comedy everyone is talking about. They're showing it in your honour evidently.'

His voice grated ever so slightly but apart from that he appeared pretty much in control. Sharon forced herself to smile. There was no point in confusing herself even more by looking for answers to questions like that. They would appear in their own good time and she would deal with them then.

'Then I'd better go and watch it.'

She left the cabin and went with him to the canteen where the film was being shown. It was one she had been wanting to see but she found it difficult to concentrate. She couldn't stop thinking about what had happened and it made her very aware of Matt sitting beside her. She was a bag of nerves by the time the film ended and the lights came on.

She sighed as everyone began to disperse. Did Matt have any idea of the problems he was causing her? She hoped not!

The three men looked marginally better when Sharon went to check on them next morning. Surprisingly, she had slept well and not even the storm roaring around the rig had woken her. It was as though her mind had simply shut down because it hadn't been able to deal with anything more. However, when she had awoken it had all come flooding back, from Matt's confession about the celibate state of his life to those sweet moments when he had held her.

She knew that she had to put what had happened into context but it wasn't easy to do that. The need to make Matt see that he had a future to look forward to was still very strong, yet she knew that he wouldn't welcome her interference.

Sandy Atkins, the young Australian, was obviously feeling well enough to try flirting with her. 'Come to soothe our fevered brows, have you, sweetheart? Do yourself a favour and start with me first. Be a shame to waste your time on that pair of no-hopers.'

He treated her to a come-hither look that made her laugh. 'I can tell you're feeling better! But I don't know about soothing your fevered brow. Isn't that Gerry's prerogative? I don't want to go treading on his toes.'

Sandy groaned. ''Struth, you're a hard-hearted woman! Leaving a fellow in Gerry's care is downright cruel. I thought you nurses were supposed to be caring and compassionate.'

'They are, but I'm not a nurse.' She grinned wickedly at him. 'I'm a paramedic, you see, and we're a tough breed!'

'You'd have to be when you consider some of the sights you must see,' one of the other men, Colin Hancock, put in. He had been the sickest out of the three and had said very little the previous day. Sharon was delighted that he was feeling well enough to take part in the conversation.

'It can get stressful at times,' she agreed. 'But it's a very rewarding job. It's great to know that you're giving people a real chance of recovery.'

'You lot do a great job!' Lee Travers, the young American, added his vote. 'I couldn't do what you do and I don't mind admitting it.'

'It's not a job that appeals to everyone,' she said quickly, feeling a bit uncomfortable about all the praise. Although she knew how vital her job was she had never considered herself to be special because she had chosen to do it. 'I wouldn't like to work on board this rig, quite frankly.'

'Oh, you get used to it,' Sandy assured her. 'It's hard work and there are drawbacks, like no drink being allowed on board and the lack of women. But we make up for that when we're on leave, don't we, fellows?'

'Uh-huh, although we might have been better staying on board after what's happened,' Colin said wryly. 'Doc Dempster said that we must have caught the plague while we were staying with Lee's family. We went camping near to where they live and we were all covered with flea bites after a couple of days. Turned out that we had pitched our tent close to a colony of prairie dogs. The doc said that they can be carriers of the disease.'

'So he explained to me,' Sharon agreed. 'I hadn't realised that bubonic plague still existed, to be honest.'

'Me neither,' Sandy chipped in. 'In fact, I'm going to have the Doc write a letter to my folks confirming what I've had because they'll never believe me when I tell them!'

They all laughed at that. Sharon looked round as the door opened and felt her heart give a small jolt of pleasure when she saw Matt. He came to join them, smiling when Sandy put in his request.

'You think your family will accuse you of telling tall tales, do you?'

'Too right they will. So I need either a letter or someone to take home with me to confirm it.' Sandy winked at her. 'How about you, sweetheart? Fancy coming back to Oz with me to back up my story? I'll be able to dine out for *years* on a tale like this so long as folk believe me!'

Sharon shook her head. 'Sorry, but I'm afraid I'm needed here. You'll just have to rely on Dr Dempster's letter to convince them.'

She glanced at Matt and was surprised by the grim expression on his face. He must have realised that she was looking at him because he made an effort to smile.

'You'll get your letter, Sandy. In fact, I might even write an article about this for one of the medical journals. I'll send you a copy if it's published.'

'Right on, Doc! The invites will be rolling in once word gets round that I'm famous. It will help make up for the fact that I can't persuade this little lady to come home with me.' He sighed. 'Still, I expect she's spoken for, otherwise you'd have snapped her up yourself.'

Sharon couldn't look at Matt. The comment had touched a raw nerve and it seemed wiser to let it pass. Matt obviously agreed because he merely smiled before he told the men that he wanted to examine them.

She left him to it. There wasn't much she could do to help and she doubted that he would want her hanging around. The helicopter bringing in the medical team would be arriving shortly and then they would be transported back to the mainland. Give it a couple of days and this whole episode would have been forgotten.

She sighed as she went to her cabin to fetch her flight suit. She wouldn't forget it in a hurry even if Matt did.

CHAPTER EIGHT

'I DON'T want you to worry unduly. It's far more difficult than you might think to catch bubonic plague. So long as you complete the course of antibiotics, and remember what to look out for, then I'm sure you'll be fine.'

'Fever, chills, headache, nausea and swellings in the lymph glands,' Sharon recited. She grinned at Grace Harding, the consultant in infectious and tropical diseases at the hospital where they had been taken. 'I've memorised all the symptoms.'

'Obviously a model patient! I wish I had more like you.' Grace carried on talking as she went to the sink and washed her hands. 'As I say, I'm not expecting you to have contracted the disease but, just to be on the safe side, I'm afraid that I am going to have to sign you off from work.'

'Oh, is that really necessary?' Sharon exclaimed in dismay, thinking of the disruption it would cause.

'Unfortunately, yes.' Grace dried her hands then came back to the desk. 'It will only be for a week and is purely a precaution, but it's essential that we keep a check on everyone who has come into contact with a disease like this. I know it's trite but it really is best to be safe rather than sorry.'

'I suppose you're right.' Sharon grimaced. 'I've not long started this job and I hate the thought of letting them down by going off sick.'

'It isn't your fault!' Grace said with a laugh, 'although I'm impressed by your dedication. Most people are delighted to be given an excuse to take time off work.'

'Maybe they are, but I love this job.' Sharon frowned as

a thought struck her. 'Does that mean that Matt will have to stay off work as well? That would make things even more difficult.'

'No. Fortunately, Matt has been vaccinated against bubonic plague so he isn't at risk.' Grace sighed as she sat down. 'How is he, by the way? I felt so sorry for him when his wife died and his daughter was injured. We used to work together at the Royal,' she added by way of explanation.

'Oh, I see. I hadn't realised that.' Sharon frowned, wondering how best to answer the question. She didn't want to betray any confidences yet she couldn't deny that she would love to know more about how Matt had been before the accident. This could be the perfect opportunity to find out.

'On the surface Matt is handling things superbly well,' she said slowly. 'He obviously adores Jessica and they have a very close and loving relationship.'

'But he's still torturing himself about what happened?' Grace smiled sadly when she saw Sharon's surprise. 'My husband and I knew Matt and Claire quite well—we often used to make up a foursome and go out together. We didn't see so much of them after they had Jessica. It was understandable, although I did suspect that Claire was getting overly protective of the child. She seemed reluctant to leave her even for a couple of hours.'

Sharon sighed. 'That must have made the situation even worse. It's no wonder Matt is so hung up on what has happened and so reluctant to accept that he should start trying to rebuild his life, instead of concentrating solely on caring for Jessica.'

'Is that what's been happening? I'm not surprised, mind, because he always did have a strong sense of duty. Fortunately, it was counter balanced by the zaniest sense of humour! Simon and I used to look forward to spending time with him and Claire, although she was a lot quieter than he was.' Grace smiled. 'Let's hope that he doesn't waste the rest of his life looking back.'

Sharon silently agreed. She thanked the doctor and left the office, wondering how she would get home. She hadn't seen Matt since they had arrived at the hospital so she had no way of knowing if he was still in the building. Bearing in mind what had happened, she didn't think it would be wise to hang around. Although Grace had assured her that there was little chance she would have contracted the disease, she felt uncomfortable at the thought of putting anyone else at risk. Maybe she should call a taxi, even though the thought of how much it would cost made her groan.

'Perfect timing! I was just coming to find you. I've hired a car to get us home. The rental company will pick it up from their local depot so I won't have to worry about getting it back here.'

She spun round as Matt came up behind her. 'I thought you must have gone home!'

'And left you here on your own?'

She grimaced when she saw him frown. 'Well, I wasn't sure what was happening. Sorry.'

He shrugged. 'Don't worry about it. I should have got a message to you sooner but I've been tied up filling in forms. You wouldn't believe the amount of paperwork that was needed!'

'Everything in triplicate and double-stamped,' she teased, following him to the exit.

'And then some! Remind me never to volunteer for any more calls like that last one, will you? My writing hand is numb.'

He pulled a face as he hauled open the door. Sharon laughed as she stepped out into the fresh morning air. The sun was shining and the air was sweetly scented by the flowers that filled the pots either side of the entrance. It was hard to believe that an hour before she had been in the middle of the North Sea, watching huge waves lapping around the oil rig.

'Oh, poor you. It's a hard life, isn't it?' she taunted.

'Watch it, cheeky! I'll make you walk home if you're not careful.'

'Probably ringing a bell and wearing a sign around my neck saying UNCLEAN,' she retorted.

'Would I do a thing like that?' He grinned as he unlocked the car.

'I refuse to answer that until I'm safely home!' she responded, sliding smartly into the car.

Matt chuckled as he got in and started the engine. 'Wise woman.'

They left the hospital and drove through the town. Matt glanced at her when the approach to the motorway appeared up ahead.

'I thought we'd take the back roads rather than the motorway, if that's OK with you. You aren't in a rush to get home, are you?'

'Not really. It would be lovely to sit back and enjoy the scenery rather than roaring along. But what about Jessica? Won't she be worrying where you are?'

'I've already spoken to her. Mum and Dad are taking her to the swimming baths so she wasn't the least concerned about what time I'd get back.' He smiled. 'I may as well make the most of having a few hours to myself.'

Amen to that! Sharon thought. It was about time that Matt put himself first for a change, and encouraging that he had done so. Maybe it marked an upturn in his attitude. The thought added an extra sparkle to the day and she smiled happily.

'What are you looking so pleased about?'

She shrugged, not daring to say too much in case he

instantly retreated into his shell. 'The day, the drive, the fact that I can't see a single drop of sea water anywhere.'

He laughed out loud. 'I take it that you won't be rushing back to that rig? But you have to admit that you got a very warm welcome.'

She laughed at his teasing. 'I don't know if it was actually *me* who warranted the welcome or the fact that I just happened to be a *woman*.'

'Don't be so modest. Those guys back there recognise a beautiful woman when they see one.'

'Thank you,' she said softly. She summoned a smile when he looked at her. 'Like most women, I enjoy being paid the odd compliment.'

'You're welcome, although I suspect that you must get your fair share of compliments, Sharon.'

His voice grated ever so slightly and she swallowed. Maybe it was her imagination but suddenly the air seemed to be charged with a tension that hadn't been apparent before. She turned to look out of the window, not sure how to deal with what was happening—if indeed anything was.

'I used to do a lot of walking in this area when I was younger.'

Once again there was that same roughness in his voice and she felt the tiny hairs all over her body stand to attention when she heard it. She made herself take a deep breath but she could hear the strain in her own voice when she replied.

'Did you? Obviously you're the outdoor type because you mentioned something about climbing as well the other day.'

'That's right. I used to spend as much time as possible out in the open air when I was at med school. I found it a good way to relax from the pressure of studying.'

His tone was back to normal once more and she breathed a sigh of relief. She was already so aware of him that her system was in danger of overloading without her tuning in to anything else.

'The pressure doesn't end when you've sat your final exams, though, does it? There's still all the pre- and post-registration training to get through.'

'Tell me about it!' He groaned. 'The hours I did as a junior houseman don't bear thinking about. Sleep became an obsession. I used to long for a day off just so I could sleep the clock round!'

'You mean you weren't living it up?' She laughed when he gave her a speaking look. 'So much for all those myths about young doctors and their partying.'

'Oh, I had my moments but that's what they were—moments. The rest of the time it was nose to the grindstone. Still, I've never regretted it so I'm not complaining. I love what I do.'

'Did Claire work with you? Is that how you met her?' she asked softly, wondering if she might be saying the wrong thing. But, surprisingly, there was no hesitation before he answered.

'Yes and no.' He laughed when he saw her confusion. 'Claire was a teacher and she worked on the children's ward, tutoring kids who needed to be in hospital long term. We didn't actually work together but we met at the hospital.'

'Oh, I see.' Sharon didn't know what else to say, funnily enough. Now that she had opened the way to more questions, she was no longer sure that she wanted to know anything else. Did she really want to hear Matt telling her how much he had loved Claire and still missed her?

The answer was a resounding *no* but before she could change the subject he continued. She steeled herself when she heard the pensive note in his voice.

'I bumped into her in the canteen one day—literally! I knocked her flying and ended up buying her lunch to make up for the one she'd dropped. We started going out together after that and six months later we got married.'

'Quite quick, really?' she said carefully, afraid of saying too much in case he guessed how difficult she was finding it to talk about the other woman.

'There was no point waiting. We knew that we wanted to be together so we went ahead.' He laughed softly. 'It took less than two months to organise the wedding, which is amazing when you think about it. But Claire was always wonderful at that kind of thing.'

Sharon managed a smile when he glanced at her. It was her own fault for starting this but it wasn't easy to hear him reminisce about his wife. 'She must have been. Most weddings take *years* to plan.'

'So I believe.' He suddenly sighed as he slowed to make a left turn. 'It all seems a long time ago now, to tell the truth. It feels as though it happened in another lifetime.'

'I suppose it does. But it's good to have memories to look back on, Matt,' she said quietly, putting aside her own feelings so that she could comfort him. What did her feelings matter? It was Matt who was suffering and she wanted to do everything she could to help him.

'Yes. But there's a very real danger of letting yourself get so obsessed by memories that you never move on. I wonder if that's what I've been doing, Sharon.'

'Maybe,' she whispered, because she was just so shocked. Her heart began to pound as she wondered why he had reached that conclusion all of a sudden. Did it have anything to do with her?

'Then maybe it's time I took a long hard look at my life and made some changes,' he said quietly.

He turned his attention to the road after that and didn't say anything more. However, that didn't mean Sharon could forget what he'd said. Her mind seemed to be overwhelmed by the thought of the changes he might be considering making to his life and whether she would be involved in them. Was that what she wanted, to be part of his future?

Yes! her heart replied joyfully, sending her into an even bigger spin. It was difficult to act normally but she tried her best as the conversation shifted to more impersonal topics. Matt was a good driver and dealt skilfully with the winding roads, but it was still a long journey. Sharon was more than happy to agree when he suggested that they should stop for an early lunch.

They found a small pub close to the river and drew up in the car park. There were tables outside so they opted to sit there and eat their lunch. Sharon ordered turkey salad sandwiches on wholemeal bread while Matt chose prawn and both of them decided on lemonade rather than anything alcoholic.

She sighed with pleasure after she had finished the last mouthful. 'That was delicious!'

'Wasn't it?' he agreed, polishing off the last bite of his sandwich. He smiled as he stared appreciatively at the river. 'What a fabulous view. I must remember this place. Jess would love it here.'

'She would. I used to love paddling in rivers when I was her—' She stopped abruptly, aghast by what she had said. 'Oh, I'm so sorry, Matt! I just didn't think.'

'Hey, don't be silly.' He covered her hand with his and his eyes were gentle. 'I don't want you thinking that you have to censor every word you say. I know that you would never deliberately say anything to hurt either Jessica or me. It just isn't in your nature to do that, Sharon.'

'It isn't, but I should have been more careful...'

He placed a gentle finger against her lips. 'Stop it! I won't have you blaming yourself when it's completely unnecessary.'

'That's how I feel about you blaming yourself for Jessica's accident.'

The words came out before she could stop them and she felt him stiffen. He removed his finger from her lips but, surprisingly, kept hold of her hand. Sharon had the strangest feeling that he needed to keep hold of it, that in some way the contact was as vital to him as breathing at that moment.

'I want to believe what you're saying, Sharon. I really do.' His voice was tortured by doubt and she bit her lip. She ached to reassure him but she knew in her heart that he had to reach the conclusion that he wasn't to blame for the accident all by himself for it to mean anything.

'I want to believe that I wasn't at fault but it's hard. I feel that I'm making excuses because I can't face the truth.'

'The *truth* is that it was an accident!' She couldn't hold back any longer. She laid her free hand on top of his, willing her conviction to flow into him. If Matt could only accept that he wasn't guilty then he could move on. She wouldn't let herself think further than that.

'Some people might call it fate, others might see it as an act of God, and I don't know who would be right. But the simple truth is that it happened and you weren't to blame. It was just Claire's time to die and I know that it doesn't make sense, and I know that it makes even less sense that Jessica was injured, but it's something you have to accept.'

She wasn't aware that she was crying until she felt the tears running down her cheeks. It didn't seem to matter all that much because how she felt wasn't the issue. It was Matt who was important, *his* feelings that needed to be considered, *his* heart that had been broken.

The tears streamed even harder down her face at that thought and she heard him mutter something as he drew her to her feet and led her away from the pub and any prying eyes. The garden ran right down to the river and he waited until they were standing on the bank before he turned her into his arms and held her so tightly that she could barely breathe let alone cry any more.

'Don't, Sharon! I never meant you to get upset like this,' he said huskily.

'What you mean is that you didn't want me to get involved,' she cried brokenly. 'Do you think I don't know that, Matt? Do you think I didn't realise that you were deliberately trying to push me away?'

'Because I never wanted this to happen!' He set her away from him so that he could look into her eyes. 'I didn't want you getting hurt!'

'I'm not hurt!' she denied, and heard him sigh.

'Then why are you crying? They aren't tears of joy, sweetheart.' He ran a finger down her cheek, smiling grimly when he saw the glisten of moisture on his skin.

She tried to pull away then, deeply hurt that he should mock her. 'No, they're not. Sorry. I've done it again, haven't I? Overstepped the mark and said something I shouldn't have said.'

'Yes. And I wish I could tell you never to do it again only…only I don't think I'm selfless enough to do that.'

She went quite still, shocked into immobility by the aching note in his voice. Somehow she found the strength to look up and the expression in his eyes at that moment made her bones turn to liquid. Matt was looking at her with a hunger which he made no attempt to disguise.

'I love it that you care what happens to me, Sharon. I know I shouldn't feel like this because I have nothing to offer you in return. But it makes me want to forget the bad things and think only about the good.'

He took a deep breath and she felt his chest rise and fall because they were standing so close. 'It makes me feel alive and it's been a long time since I felt like this…a very, very long time…'

His voice tailed off because there was no way he could carry on speaking while he was kissing her. Sharon wrapped her arms around his neck and clung to him while she returned the kiss with one that was tinged with desperation. If there was a way to convince him by simple osmosis that this was right then she would do so!

His lips plundered hers hungrily, greedily, as though he was starving for the taste and feel of hers. Maybe he was because it was a long time since he had admitted to his own needs.

Sharon simply opened her heart to him, not trying to hold back any reserves of emotion. It was pointless doing that, silly to play games. This wasn't a contest to see which of them needed the other most. She wanted to give him everything she had it in her power to give and hope that it helped him, healed him. Love was like that, though. A wonderful chance to give as well as receive.

The thought slid into her mind and brought with it only pleasure, oddly enough. She loved Matt and that explained so many things that had happened of late. He must have felt her smile because he drew back and looked at her.

'Sharon?'

'Matthew?' she countered, not wanting to make her confession just yet. She loved him, but until she had grown used to the idea she didn't intend to share it with him. In a funny way it seemed to lend an extra sweetness to what was happening, a sense of anticipation that could only be bettered when it finally reached its rightful conclusion…

She shivered and he smiled when he felt the ripple run through her. 'I won't ask what that was all about!'

He bestowed one last kiss on her then deliberately stepped back. 'I think we should pay for our lunch and get out of here before we cause a real stir, don't you?'

'I expect you're right.' She reached up and kissed him again, smiling when he immediately returned the favour. 'I thought you were determined to keep me at a distance?'

'A man can change his mind, can't he? It isn't only a woman's right to do that in these enlightened times.' A shadow suddenly darkened his face. 'Sharon, I don't know if—'

'Don't!' She stopped him by the simple expedient of a well-placed kiss. 'We aren't doing anything wrong, Matt. We are both young, free and single. Well, I'm *young*, free and single, anyway.'

'Are you implying that I'm old, Miss Lennard?' He glowered when she laughed.

'If the hat fits…' She scooted out of the way when he made a lunge for her, waggling her fingers at him as she headed for the car. 'Didn't you say something about paying the bill?'

'I shall have my revenge so watch out, *young* lady!' he warned.

'Ooh, I'm really scared!' She carried on to the car while he went into the pub. He wasn't gone long and she watched him walking towards her while her heart overflowed with love. He looked a world removed from the man she had met a few weeks earlier, but she wasn't foolish enough to believe that he was completely over the past.

She smiled determinedly as he opened the car door, refusing to admit to any doubts. She had to be confident enough for both of them that the future would turn out how she hoped it would.

They kept up an easy conversation while they drove, but by the time they arrived at her house Sharon was feeling positively weak with tension. Matt hadn't said anything to imply that he was hoping they could continue what they had started by the river, but that hadn't stopped her mind running riot.

'Would you like to come in for coffee?' she offered, her heart knocking against her ribs as she wondered how he would interpret the offer.

'I'm not the least bit interested in coffee,' he replied in a tone that sounded like dark brown silk.

'Neither am I,' she confessed, then clamped a hand over her unruly mouth.

He grinned. 'Really?'

She blushed furiously but steadfastly met his eyes. 'We both know that suggesting coffee was only a polite way of asking if you wanted to carry on where we left off before.'

'We do.' He leant over and kissed her hungrily then drew back. 'And I would love to do just that.'

'But?' She gave a forced little laugh because she had already anticipated his refusal. Matt was going to tell her that he didn't think it was a good idea, that it wouldn't be wise, that...

'*But* I have to go into work to write up my report. I promised that I'd do it this afternoon and it's almost three o'clock now.' He kissed her again, lingeringly and in a way that made her doubts evaporate in an instant. 'I don't want to be clock-watching when we're together. I want us to have all the time in the world to enjoy it.'

'Oh!' There wasn't anything else she could say because her mind seemed to have gone into a tail-spin on hearing that.

'Oh, indeed. So, if I can arrange it, would you like to go out to dinner tonight? I'm sure Mum wouldn't mind taking charge of Jessica for another evening if I asked her.'

'I...um...yes, I'd like that.' She paused as a thought struck her. 'Do you think it might be better if we ate here rather than in a restaurant, bearing in mind what's happened?'

'Much better, although there's no danger whatsoever that you've contracted bubonic plague.' He treated her to another deliciously thorough kiss. 'However, if we eat here then we won't have to worry about shocking the other diners, will we?' he explained wickedly, laughing when she gasped.

'No,' she agreed weakly, then reluctantly opened the car door. 'I'd better let you go. I'll expect you around seven, if that's all right?'

'Fine.' He caught hold of her hand and pulled her towards him. His kiss was everything she could have wished for so that it felt as though she were floating when she finally stepped onto the pavement. Sharon watched him drive away, enveloped in a delicious haze. Maybe she should pinch herself to prove that she wasn't dreaming.

She did so and it didn't change a thing. Matt *had* kissed her and told her that he wanted to try and rebuild his life. Maybe he hadn't actually said that he saw her as an important part of his future, but surely he had implied it?

The first doubt crept in before she could stop it but she deliberately forced it to the back of her mind. Somehow she got through the rest of the day, keeping herself busy by cleaning the house and making a complicated chicken dish for dinner. After that, it was time for a shower then the thorny problem of what she should wear. She tried on every outfit in her wardrobe and promptly discarded them because nothing seemed right. She wanted to look her very best that night for Matt.

The sound of the telephone ringing just before seven had her hurrying into the hall, and her heart leapt when she heard Matt's voice. That delicious haze seemed to have enveloped her again so that it was a moment before she realised what he was saying.

'Jessica?' she repeated. 'She's been taken to hospital? But why? What's happened?'

'I'm not sure.' He barely gave her time to finish. 'All I know is that she's in a great deal of pain. I'm sorry, Sharon, but we'll have to forget about dinner. I'm on my way to the hospital with her right now.'

He hung up and Sharon slowly replaced the receiver. She went back to her bedroom and looked at the heap of clothes spread across the bed. She certainly didn't blame Matt for putting his daughter before a dinner date. What hurt was the fact that he hadn't asked her to go to the hospital with him. It made her see how foolish it was to hope there was a place for her in his life.

Matt had everything he needed—a daughter he loved, a job that fulfilled him and a store of wonderful memories. He didn't need her or her love to make his life complete.

CHAPTER NINE

THE following week off work seemed to drag. Sharon tried to fill in the hours as best she could, but there was only so much she could find to do. She cleaned the bungalow until everywhere gleamed and annihilated every weed in the tiny garden, but time still hung heavily.

Matt phoned to tell her that Jessica was home from hospital. It appeared that the little girl had suffered a severe urinary tract infection but she had now recovered. He didn't invite Sharon to visit the child neither did she offer. He'd had his chance to involve her further in his life and hadn't taken it.

It was a mixed blessing when she was able to return to work. It was good to have something to focus on but worrying to wonder if she could cope with being around Matt all the time. She loved him but her initial delight on realising it had faded. She was terrified that she might unwittingly reveal her feelings because she knew how he would react.

Mike welcomed her back in his usual irreverent manner. 'Here she is at last, Little Miss Lucky. Not only did she get an all-expenses-paid stay at one of the most exclusive resorts in the world, but she got a week off work to recover from it! Come on, Shaz, tell us your secret—how did you manage it?'

'Some people just have the knack of being in the right place at the right time. You've either got it or you haven't, I'm afraid,' she replied, treating him to a suitably regal smile.

'Thank heavens I'm one of the ones who *haven't* got it,'

Beth chipped in. 'I don't know about exclusive but I wouldn't fancy being on an oil rig, thank you very much, with or without bubonic plague!'

Sharon laughed. 'Why ever not? I mean, there you are in the middle of the North Sea with a gale-force wind blowing…'

'Don't!' Beth shuddered. 'I can't bear to imagine what it was like. Still, at least you had Matt there with you. That must have been some consolation.'

Sharon turned away when Beth gave her an old-fashioned look, afraid of what might be written on her face at that moment. Fortunately, Bert arrived just then and she was spared having to reply as he bombarded her with questions. By the time Beth left a short time later, she had forgotten about it.

Sharon wasn't sorry because she would have found it difficult to have come up with a reply. Had it been a consolation to have Matt there? Or had it made an already difficult situation worse? Would she have realised how she felt about him if they hadn't spent that time together?

It was just too confusing so she tried not to dwell on it. Fortunately, it wasn't long before they had their first call of the day. A lorry had run out of control whilst travelling down a steep section of the M62 motorway. There were a number of cars involved and long tailbacks of traffic because it had happened during the morning rush hour. The ambulances were having problems getting to the site of the accident which was why they had been asked to attend.

Andy circled the area several times, looking for a suitable landing site. 'The traffic's still moving down there. I can't take the risk of trying to land until I'm sure nothing is going to get in the way.'

'I'll get on to Mike and have him patch us through to the police,' Matt informed him. Sharon listened while he spoke to base then a moment later the officer in charge came on the radio.

Matt quickly explained their predicament and was assured that the traffic would be brought to a standstill immediately. He sighed as he stared down at the wreckage strewn across the westbound carriageway.

'Looks like it's going to be pretty grim down there. Sharon, you act as triage nurse so we can sort out the most badly injured and deal with them first. OK?'

'Fine,' she assured him, keeping a tight rein on her emotions. Matt had said very little to her that morning, apart from asking her how she was. It was obvious that he was deliberately setting some distance between them and although she wasn't surprised, she was hurt. Did Matt regret having opened up to her the other day?

The crackle of the radio as the police officer confirmed they were cleared to land was a welcome distraction from such unhappy thoughts. Sharon focused on what she had to do as Andy landed the helicopter on the carriageway. Matt flung open the doors then glanced back.

'We all know what we have to do so just be careful. Don't go taking any chances.' His gaze seemed to linger on Sharon before he jumped down from the helicopter and ran towards the nearest vehicle.

Sharon snatched up her medical bag and quickly followed him. She wouldn't allow herself to believe that Matt had directed that warning at her. She wasn't silly enough to imagine that he cared. The trouble was that her head was telling her one thing while her heart was telling her something entirely different. Oh, hell!

She managed to push it to the back of her mind as she stopped beside a car near the front of the pile-up. There was a couple in it, both conscious and able to respond coherently when she spoke to them. It was obvious that they were in no immediate danger so, after a brief word of reassurance, she ran to the next vehicle, which was a white van.

The driver was unhurt apart from a cut on his cheek, but one of the men who had been travelling in the back of the van was in a bad way. He had been thrown onto the carriageway when the rear doors had burst open and Sharon could tell immediately that he had suffered severe head injuries.

'How is he?' Matt demanded when she called him over.

'Not good. Both pupils fixed and dilated.' She pointed to the man's left ear from where a stream of clear, watery fluid was leaking. 'That's cerebrospinal fluid by the look of it.'

'Doesn't look too good.' Matt sounded grim as he quickly began to examine him. 'Looks like there's some internal damage, too. Let's get him on a drip and send him on his way. There's little we can do for him here.'

They quickly prepared the man for immediate transfer to hospital. There were plans in place to deal with major incidents like this and a number of hospitals in the area had been put on standby to treat the casualties. Within a very short time the man was on his way to a specialist unit in Manchester.

Sharon was already working her way through the vehicles by the time Andy took off. Bert was accompanying the patient and they would return once he had been handed over. Fortunately, one of the ground ambulances had managed to get through the traffic so she and another paramedic carried on prioritising treatment for the most severely injured. It was hard to make people understand what they were doing because everyone was upset and wanted help, but it was vital that those in most urgent need of treatment were seen first.

'Can you take a look at my daughter?'

Sharon swung round as someone grabbed her arm, putting out a steadying hand when the woman who had accosted her swayed. 'Sit down,' she instructed, trying to lead her to the banking at the side of the motorway.

'No, no! I'm all right. It's my little girl…please, you've got to come!'

The woman turned and ran frantically back up the carriageway. Sharon looked at the other paramedic, who shrugged.

'Better take a look. I'll carry on here.'

Sharon didn't hesitate any longer before she quickly followed the woman to her car. It was right at the back of the pile-up and appeared to be undamaged, so she had no idea what could have happened.

'I don't know what's wrong with her. One minute Jane was perfectly all right then I looked in the mirror after I'd slammed on my brakes and she was like this!'

The woman wrenched open the door while she was speaking and Sharon's heart sank when she saw the little girl. It was obvious that the child was having problems breathing because her lips were blue.

'Help me get her out,' she instructed, unfastening the child's seat belt. They laid her on the carriageway and Sharon quickly checked for a pulse, feeling deeply relieved when she found one.

She quickly checked the child's mouth for any obstructions then bagged her—using a hand-held air pump to blow air into her lungs. However, it was obvious after a few seconds that nothing was happening.

'There must be a blockage…something stopping the air getting into her lungs,' she told the anxious mother.

She opened the child's mouth again but there was no sign of what was causing the obstruction. If something was stopping the air reaching the child's lungs then it had to be stuck lower down in her throat.

'I'm sure that something is blocking her airway. Could she have swallowed anything?' she asked the mother.

'I don't think so... Oh, she had some sweets with her...humbugs! Her grandmother gave them to her before we left this morning. I told Jane not to eat them but maybe she did!'

Sharon didn't wait to hear any more. She hauled the little girl into an upright position and performed the Heimlich manoeuvre on her, pressing her clenched fist into the child's abdomen to try and dislodge the sweet. However, it soon became apparent that it wasn't going to work.

'What have we got?' Matt suddenly appeared and she looked at him in relief.

'I think she's swallowed a sweet. I can't shift it and I can't get any air into her. There's no point trying to intubate her because we won't be able to get the tube past the blockage.'

'Then we can't afford to waste any more time.' He turned to the child's terrified mother and there was a wealth of compassion in his voice. 'Your daughter is going to die if we don't do something immediately. I know this is going to look brutal but it's the only way to save her life. Do you understand?'

'Yes! I don't care what you do just don't let her die!'

The woman was sobbing now and Sharon felt very sorry for her, but she couldn't allow her feelings to get in the way of doing her job. She had guessed what Matt was planning so quickly found some antiseptic and swabbed the child's throat. An incision would have to be made into the little girl's trachea and a tube inserted to allow the air to flow into her lungs.

It was all over in record time—Matt administered a local anaesthetic, made the incision and inserted a tracheostomy tube. Sharon taped it in place, relieved to see that the child's colour had returned almost to normal.

'Thank you. I don't know what to say except that.' The mother could barely speak. It was obvious that she was deeply shocked by what had happened. Matt helped her to her feet while the ambulance crew loaded the child on board to transfer her to hospital.

'Jane should be fine now so try not to worry too much,' he assured her, helping her into the ambulance. He sighed as he watched it driving away. 'Not that there's the slightest chance of her taking any notice. It's par for the course when you have a child, I'm afraid.'

Sharon didn't say anything because she wasn't qualified to comment. She didn't have any children, although she could imagine how she would have felt if it had been Jessica being treated just now. A lump came to her throat at that thought and she turned away abruptly.

'Sharon?'

She didn't even pause as she went back to work. She would concentrate on her job and nothing else. At the end of the day that was all she and Matt had in common. He had his life to lead and she had hers. The only point where they crossed was during working hours.

They were all exhausted by the time they returned to base. There had been six fatalities and ten people seriously injured. Five of those had been taken to hospital by helicopter and they could only hope that would have increased their chances of recovery, although there were no guarantees. Even doing their best sometimes wasn't enough. Sharon suspected that explained the rather sombre mood on board the helicopter when it landed.

'Good work, everyone. We'll have a debriefing in the office in ten minutes' time.' Matt was first to leave the helicopter as usual but he hung back to wait for her to alight. He drew her aside as one of the mechanics came over to speak to Andy.

'Are you all right? It was pretty rough out there...'

She cut him off, not wanting him to think that she expected special treatment. 'I'm fine. It isn't the first time that I've attended an incident like that nor will it be the last, I imagine. I'm quite capable of dealing with it.'

'I'm sure you are. And I didn't mean to imply that you weren't,' he said stiffly.

'Then there's no problem, is there?' She gave him a tight smile then went inside. Maybe she shouldn't have been so brusque but it wasn't easy to deal with this situation. Matt didn't need her, didn't want her, didn't intend to make a place for her in his life. Those were the facts and she had to face them, painful though it was.

The debriefing didn't take very long. They were each required to write up an incident report as well so Sharon took her lunch into the garden and wrote hers there. She had just finished when she heard the sound of a child's laughter and looked up to see Jessica bowling down the path in her wheelchair.

'Surprise!' The little girl laughed in delight when she heard Sharon gasp. 'I knew you'd be surprised to see me: I told Granny you would be.'

'You were right, too. It is a surprise but a lovely one. How are you? Your daddy told me that you'd been poorly but that you were better now,' Sharon explained, getting up to hug the little girl.

'I had a ury-trak infession,' Jessica told her importantly.

Sharon tried not to laugh. 'So I believe, sweetheart. It must have been horrible for you.'

'It was, but the nurses in the hospital were nice.' Jessica frowned. 'I asked Daddy if you could come and visit me, Sharon, but he said that you were too busy.'

Had he indeed?

It was on the tip of Sharon's tongue to explain that she would have loved to have visited her, only she knew it would be wrong to cause friction between father and daughter.

'Did he? Anyway, it's lovely to see you, but what are you doing here?' she asked, diplomatically changing the subject even though she had no intention of letting Matt get away with that. She was a grown woman and could make up her own mind whether or not she had time to spare!

'Granny forgot to take the front door key with her when we went out this morning,' Jessica explained as a tall, silver-haired woman, who bore a striking resemblance to Matt, appeared.

'One of the hazards of getting older, I'm afraid. You start forgetting things left, right and centre,' the woman observed cheerfully. 'I'm Eileen Dempster, Matthew's mother, and you must be Sharon. I've heard so much about you, my dear. It's lovely to meet you at long last!'

Sharon laughed as they shook hands. 'I don't know if I like the sound of that!'

'Oh, it's been all good, I assure you.' The older woman looked at her granddaughter. 'You've made a big impression on Jessica. She never stops talking about you.'

'She's a lovely child,' Sharon replied sincerely, watching the little girl manoeuvre her wheelchair along the path so that she could look at a butterfly which had landed on a bush.

'She is. She has her father's interest in everything that goes on around her as well as his sense of fun. It's quite remarkable in the circumstances, really.'

'She's fortunate to have Matt as her father. He tries so hard to give her a normal life.'

'He does. But sometimes I can't help wishing that he would spend a bit more time thinking about himself.' Eileen Dempster smiled complacently when Sharon looked at her. 'A typical mother's reaction, my dear. It's very difficult to take a balanced view where your own child is concerned.'

Sharon frowned, wondering why she had the feeling that the woman was trying to tell her something. She shrugged it aside as Jessica came back.

'Have you asked her yet, Granny?'

'Why don't you do it, darling?' the older woman countered.

'Asked me what?' Sharon queried, looking from one to the other. 'This all sounds very mysterious!'

'It's Daddy's birthday on Sunday and we're having a party for him, a surprise party 'cos he doesn't know anything about it!' Jessica explained excitedly. It was obvious how thrilled she was by the thought of springing a surprise on her father, and Sharon laughed.

'I'd love to see Matt's face when he finds out what you've done,' she said without thinking.

'Oh, good. That's one question answered, then. I was hoping that you would come, my dear,' Eileen inserted smoothly, much to Sharon's dismay. She carried on before Sharon could say anything. 'Now, Jessica, tell Sharon what other surprise you have planned for Daddy's birthday.'

'I'm going to bake him a cake. A birthday cake with candles. He's thirty-eight so it will have to be a really *big* cake to fit them all on!'

'Um, I'm sure he'll be thrilled,' Sharon said weakly, because she had a feeling that she knew what was coming.

'He will if it turns out.' Eileen gave an amused laugh. 'And that's where we are hoping that you'll step in, my dear.'

'Oh, but I don't—' she began, only Jessica interrupted her.

'Will you help me make it, Sharon? Granny doesn't know how to bake cakes, you see, and I told her about the cake you'd made when we came to your house, so she said why didn't I ask you to help.' The little girl caught hold of Sharon's hand. 'You can't have a birthday party without a cake and candles, can you?'

'Perhaps you could buy one,' she suggested lamely, knowing before Jessica shook her head how that idea would be received.

'It wouldn't be the same! I want to make the cake myself for Daddy and ice it and put the candles on it.' The child looked beseechingly at her. 'Please, Sharon, please, *please*, say that you'll help me!'

It would have needed a harder heart than hers to withstand the pleading look on the little girl's face. Sharon gave a small sigh, knowing that she was probably making a huge mistake. Matt had made it plain that he wanted her to stay out of his life so he certainly wouldn't appreciate her input into his birthday party.

'All right, then, I'll help you, if you're sure it's what you want,' she said before common sense got the better of her.

Jessica gave a squeal of excitement. 'Yes!'

'That's very kind of you, my dear. I make no bones about the fact that I'm a complete dunce when it comes to culinary matters.' Eileen Dempster smiled calmly at her so that Sharon couldn't explain why she had the funniest feeling that she had been cleverly manipulated in some way.

She drove such a fanciful notion from her mind by concentrating instead on the practicalities of what they were planning. 'I've got everything we need to bake the cake, but how are we going to manage it without Matt suspecting what's going on?'

'Oh, that's all covered. His father is going to take him off for the day. Robert has come up with this story about wanting Matt to go with him to view a cottage we're thinking of buying.' Eileen laughed. 'It isn't a lie because we are thinking about buying a base in England. We just aren't thinking of buying one in such a far-flung part of the country! Robert assures me that it will take the best part of the afternoon to drive there and back.'

Sharon shook her head in admiration. 'You've thought of everything, haven't you?'

'Oh, I try. Despite my aversion to cooking, I like to think that I'm a good mother. I definitely have Matt's welfare at heart, shall we say.'

Once again Sharon had the feeling that there was something she was missing. However, just at that moment Matt himself appeared. Her heart sank when she saw the grim expression on his face as he came striding towards them.

'What's wrong?' he demanded. 'Andy just told me that you were here.'

'Nothing is wrong, darling. Well, not really. I just forgot to take the house key with me this morning when we went out.' Eileen opened her bag. 'I could have sworn I'd picked it up off the hall table… Why, here it is! It must have been in my bag all the time. How silly of me. Still, no harm done, is there?'

She turned to Sharon and winked. 'It's been lovely meeting you, my dear. Maybe we'll meet again some time soon.'

Sharon murmured something appropriate, although she wasn't blind to the speed with which Matt ushered his mother and daughter away. Was he afraid that Eileen might have issued an invitation to her if she'd had the chance? That would never have done!

Frankly, she had worked herself up into such a temper that she made a beeline for him when he came back. 'Would you mind explaining why you told Jessica that I was too busy to visit her in hospital?'

'Because I thought it was for the best.' He didn't try to excuse his actions. 'I don't want her getting too fond of you, Sharon. I explained that once before.'

'You did. Silly of me to think that the situation might have changed, wasn't it?'

She saw a rim of colour edge his cheekbones and smiled thinly even though her heart was aching. 'What *was* that all about the other day, Matt? Was it a sudden aberration that caused you to consider making changes to your life?'

'I can't see any point discussing this. I was wrong to behave the way I did and I apologise if I misled you—'

'Yes, you did! And you can keep your apology. It doesn't mean a thing. It certainly doesn't give you a licence to pretend that you never told me that you wanted to make love to me!'

'Sharon, this is neither the time nor the place for a discussion like this,' he said repressively, but she was too hurt and too angry to care.

'I agree, but seeing as this is the only place we see one another then there aren't very many options. I just want to know what happened, Matt. Why did you change your mind? Was it because when it finally came down to it you realised that no one could ever mean as much to you as Claire did?'

'My reasons are not something I intend to discuss. I made a mistake and I've apologised for it. That's as far as I intend to go, Sharon.'

His tone was harsh yet beneath the grittiness she heard the pain it held. It struck her that Matt was finding the situation as difficult to deal with as she was, although for markedly different reasons. How he must hate to be constantly reminded of the lapse he had made that day. Each time he saw her he must be forced to recall how close he had come to betraying Claire's memory.

Sharon took a deep breath, realising that she couldn't bear to know that he was suffering because of her. 'Then I shall just have to accept your apology and leave it at that, won't I?'

His face contorted with sudden pain. 'I'm sorry, Sharon, but I honestly and truly believe that it's for the best.'

She didn't wait to hear anything else. There was no point. She left him in the garden and went back inside. She would do as he wanted and not mention what had happened again, even though she would never forget it. How could she? She loved him. Never had three little words lain so heavily in anyone's heart.

CHAPTER TEN

SUNDAY arrived and Sharon got up with less than her usual enthusiasm. It was a glorious day so her mood couldn't be blamed on the weather. Eileen Dempster had phoned the previous evening and asked her to be at Matt's house just after twelve, but she was having serious doubts about what she had agreed to. She didn't need a crystal ball to tell her that Matt would be less than pleased about her involvement in the preparations for his birthday party, but she simply couldn't think of a way to back out.

She stared at herself in the bathroom mirror after she had showered, seeing the shadows in her eyes. Love certainly wasn't easy. It didn't conveniently go away when there was no chance of it being reciprocated, neither could she switch it on and off like a tap when she chose to. It was there all the time—at the back of her mind while she was working, at the forefront when she wasn't.

It made her realise how difficult it was going to be working with Matt. Maybe it would be best for both of them if she found a new job. She didn't want to leave the air ambulance service but the thought of being constantly put through the emotional wringer was much worse. With a new job and new people around her, she would be able to get on with her life, although she knew that she would never forget Matt.

It had been a difficult decision to make and Sharon's heart was heavy as she dressed. She chose a cotton print dress in shades of amber and gold that perfectly set off her russet hair. Dark brown mascara and a slick of coppery lipstick completed her outfit and she was quite pleased with the results when she looked in the mirror again. Even though it felt as though her heart was breaking, nobody could tell.

She loaded everything into the car and set off. It didn't take long to reach Matt's house, although she had a bit of fright when she saw his car outside. She found a phone box and dialled his number, ready to hang up immediately if he answered. However, it was Jessica who answered and informed her that Daddy and Gramps had gone out in her grandfather's car. Then she demanded to know when Sharon would be arriving.

Sharon drove back to the house, smiling when she recounted the tale to Matt's mother. 'I felt a real fool, skulking around in that phone box!'

Eileen chuckled. 'I can imagine. I really appreciate you doing this, Sharon. And I'm sure that Matt will appreciate it, too, once he gets over his initial shock.'

Sharon had her doubts about that. She had already made up her mind that she wouldn't be there when Matt got home, although she decided not to say anything to his mother just yet. Instead, she let Jessica help her carry the baking equipment into the kitchen, carefully balancing the cardboard box across the arms of the child's wheelchair.

'Right, first things first, young lady. We need clean hands before we do anything else.'

Jessica obediently hurried away to wash her hands and came back a few minutes later. By that time, Sharon had commandeered a coffee-table from the sitting room and had brought it into the kitchen to put the scales on so that they were at the right height for Jessica to use.

'I want you to weigh the butter and the sugar for me and put them in this big bowl,' she explained to the child. 'I've written how much of each you need on this piece of paper.'

Jessica carefully weighed out the ingredients, her tongue peeping between her lips as she virtually counted out the grains of sugar one by one to make sure that she got exactly the right amount.

Eileen smiled tenderly as she watched her granddaughter. 'She's been so excited all morning. I'm sure Matt must have suspected that something was going on, but he pretended not to notice.'

'It must have been difficult, stopping Jessica saying anything,' Sharon remarked, keeping a careful watch on what the child was doing.

'Oh, Jessica is rather good at keeping secrets.'

Eileen smiled complacently before she went out into the garden. Sharon was left with the impression that there was something going on that she was unaware of. However, there was no time to worry about it with Jessica needing her constant attention.

It was a pleasant if rather messy afternoon. Flour got spilled and one egg landed on the floor rather than in the mixing bowl but it didn't really matter. It was obvious that Jessica was having fun and that she was taking note of everything that Sharon told her.

The cake mixture was ready at last so they spooned it into the tin and carefully slid it into the oven. 'It's going to take about half an hour to bake, maybe a bit longer,' Sharon warned the child. 'Then we'll have to let the cake cool down before we can ice it. Did you remember to ask Granny to buy the candles?'

'I helped her choose them.' Jessica went to the dresser and opened one of the cupboards. She handed a pink-and-white striped bag to Sharon. 'I told Granny that we had to have blue candles because Daddy's a boy.'

'They're lovely. And so many of them, too!' Sharon chuckled. She would love to see Matt's face when he saw the cake.

A wave of pain washed over her when she realised that wasn't going to happen. He had made it plain that he didn't want her around so she would make sure that she had left before he arrived home. It just seemed to highlight that she had been right to decide to find another job. It would be too painful to be around him on a daily basis and know that she could never be part of his life.

It took another hour before the cake was finally ready. Jessica stared at it wonderment. 'It's beautiful…really, really beautiful!' she declared, studying the dripping yellow icing and rows of blue candles that adorned it. She suddenly flung her arms around Sharon's hips and hugged her. 'Thank you, Sharon. Daddy will be so pleased!'

'You're welcome, poppet.' Sharon hugged her back, smiling when she felt the thin little arms tighten around her. 'You'll squeeze me to death like that. What a grip!'

She was still laughing when the back door suddenly opened. She looked up, expecting to see Eileen, and felt her smile freeze when she saw Matt standing there instead. There was a moment when neither of them said anything then Eileen appeared behind him.

'You're back early, darling. Did you manage to find the cottage?'

'Yes.' Matt's tone was clipped although his mother seemed oblivious to it. Sharon wasn't, though, and her heart sank as she wondered what he was going to say about her being there.

'You'll have to tell me what you thought about it later.' Eileen didn't give him time to say anything as she briskly shooed him to the door. 'Off you go now. You're banned from the kitchen. Go and wait in the sitting room and we'll call you when we're ready.'

He went with obvious ill grace. Sharon grimaced as she quickly began loading all the baking equipment back into the box. 'I'd better go.' She glanced at Jessica and lowered her voice. 'I don't think Matt was very pleased to see me here and I don't want to ruin his birthday.'

'Nonsense! He was just a bit surprised, that's all.' Eileen whisked the box out of her hands and plonked it on the draining-board. 'We won't hear of you leaving, will we, Jessica?'

Sharon groaned when the little girl added her eager assurances that she must stay. She knew how disappointed Jessica would be if she refused. It placed her in a very awkward position because she also knew how much Matt resented her presence.

She did her best to behave as though nothing out of the ordinary had happened as she helped Eileen lay out the tea in the garden, but all the time she kept wondering what Matt was going to say. In the event, he behaved impeccably, praising Jessica for the cake and thanking Sharon for helping her to make it. However, she knew that it was all an act and that he must be inwardly seething. She could hardly wait to make her escape once the candles had been blown out and the cake had been cut.

'I really must go,' she said, quickly standing up. 'It's been lovely but I must get home.'

'Thank you so much for coming, my dear.' Eileen turned to her husband. 'Don't you think it was simply lovely of Sharon to volunteer to help, Robert?'

'Lovely,' Robert Dempster replied dryly, winking at Sharon. 'Although, knowing my wife, *volunteer* isn't the word I'd have used!'

Sharon laughed politely then quickly said goodbye to an obviously disappointed Jessica.

'You will come and see me again, Sharon?' the child pleaded, clinging to her hand. 'Promise?'

'I'll try,' she hedged, conscious that Matt was listening. He stood up when she turned to leave and smiled at her, although there was a glint in his eyes that told her it would be a mistake to take his mood at face value.

'I'll see you out.'

'There's no need—' she began.

'Of course there is.' He took hold of her arm and quickly steered her towards the house. But instead of taking her straight to the front door, he detoured into the study and shut the door. 'Would you care to explain what has been going on here?'

'What's to explain?' She gave a little shrug, striving for nonchalance and failing miserably. It annoyed her because it was unfair that he was blaming her when none of this had been her fault.

'Your mother asked me if I would help Jessica make you a birthday cake. If you have a problem with that, I suggest you discuss it with her,' she said curtly.

'My problem isn't with my mother because I know exactly what she's up to. She is trying her hand at match-making.' He smiled thinly when Sharon gasped. 'You had no idea you'd been set up?'

'No! Why should I have had?' she exclaimed, her heart sinking when she remembered the feeling she'd had earlier that she'd been missing something.

'I just thought that it might have struck you as odd that she went to such lengths to get you here.'

'Well, it didn't. She told me that it was meant to be a surprise for you and I believed her. You can make what you like of that because I really don't care!'

She tried to push past him but it was a mistake to do that. As soon as her hands encountered the muscular contours of his chest they seemed to lose momentum. She no longer wanted to push him away but draw him closer, hold him and keep on holding him until he realised what a mistake he was making by driving her out of his life!

'Oh, Sharon, you don't make it easy.'

His voice was little more than a whisper yet she heard the words as clearly as though he had shouted them out loud. She went quite still, not even daring to breathe. When she felt his hands glide up her bare arms in the lightest, gentlest of caresses she still didn't react. She had been here before, had let herself hope for the impossible, then had watched her dreams being shattered. She didn't think she could bear to play this scene a second time yet she didn't have the will-power to stop it happening.

When his mouth found hers she tried to hold back her response but it was impossible to control the rush of emotions she felt. The taste and feel of his lips seemed to unlock all the love she felt for him so that suddenly she was kissing him back. Maybe it was a mistake and she would regret it later but there was no way that she could pretend right then.

'Sharon, Sharon.' He murmured her name over and over again between kisses, his voice hoarse with a need he couldn't hide. Sharon clung to him while he painted her face with kisses, murmuring soft little endearments as she felt his lips skimming over her cheeks and brow. When his lips found hers again, she wound her arms around his neck, glorying in the feel of his strong body pressed against hers. Whether Matt was willing to admit it or not, he wanted her!

He was breathing heavily when he finally raised his head. Sharon could see the heat of passion in his eyes and her heart seemed to roll over inside her. Suddenly she was filled with conviction that they could work things out if they tried.

'Matt, I—'

'Daddy! Daddy, where *are* you?'

The sound of Jessica's voice made them both jump. Matt took a deep breath then abruptly let her go. Sharon felt a wave of pain wash over her as she watched all the warmth and passion fading from his eyes.

'I'm sorry, Sharon. I shouldn't have done that. I don't know what came over me.'

She turned away, terrified that she would break down. That was the last thing she wanted to do, to let him see how hurt she was. That Matt should *apologise* for the fact that he had wanted her was almost more than she could bear.

Her legs felt like lead as she made her way down the hall. Matt reached past her to open the front door and for a moment it looked as though he was going to say something, only she didn't give him the chance.

'Goodbye, Matt.'

There was a note of finality in her voice and she saw an expression of intense pain cross his face when he heard it. There was a grating quality to his voice when he replied. 'Goodbye, Sharon.'

He touched her lightly on the arm then moved aside. Sharon left the house and hurried down the path. She could feel the sun warm on her face, smell the scent of the flowers, taste the salt of her own tears as they poured down her face, and knew that she must still be alive. It was just on the inside, where it really mattered, that she felt completely dead.

The next few weeks were a nightmare. Sharon had hoped that the situation would ease once the new rosters came into force and Matt changed shifts. However, even though she saw him only fleetingly in passing each day, she found every encounter extremely stressful.

When a job with her old team in London was advertised in one of the journals, she decided to apply for it. She couldn't keep putting herself through this torment day after day. She had to make a new life for herself and she would never do that if she stayed around Matt, wishing for the impossible to happen.

She phoned for an application form on her day off and, as luck would have it, was put through to her old boss. He was delighted when he discovered why she was phoning and immediately set a date for her to be interviewed.

When Sharon hung up she knew that the interview was a formality and that the job would be hers. It should have been a consolation to know that she wouldn't have to face the present situation much longer, but when she went back into work the following day, it didn't feel like that. Her feelings for Matt wouldn't go away just because she would be living at the opposite end of the country.

It was such a painful thought that when she passed Matt in the corridor on her way to the staffroom she completely ignored him. She just couldn't pretend that everything was normal any longer. Her heart was breaking—how normal was that?

It was just unfortunate that Mike happened to witness what had gone on and followed her into the staffroom. 'Have you and Matt had some sort of falling-out? I detected a definite chill in the air just now.'

'It's a good job that you don't do the weather forecasts is all I can say,' she said lightly, hoping to deflect any more questions.

'Meaning that I imagined it?' Mike shrugged. 'Maybe, but I don't think so. I'm not the only one to have noticed a certain atmosphere of late. Andy remarked only the other day that there's a definite tension in the air whenever you and Matt bump into one another.'

He treated her to a conspiratorial smile. 'Come on, you can tell your Uncle Mike—you and Matt have something going for you, don't you?'

'No.' Sharon made a great production out of putting her bag in her locker so that Mike couldn't see her face. 'You're way off the mark. There's nothing whatsoever going on between me and Matthew Dempster, I assure you!'

She slammed her locker shut, hoping that had put an end to Mike's prying. Although he meant well, she had no in-

tention of discussing what had gone on between her and
Matt with anyone else.

A movement by the door suddenly caught her attention
and she felt herself go cold when she saw that Matt must
have come into the room without them noticing. She felt
quite sick when she realised that he must have overheard
everything that had been said.

'Oh, right. Fine. Well, I'd better go and see what needs
to be done,' Mike muttered, shooting an uneasy look at
Matt. He hurried out of the room, discreetly closing the
door behind him as he left. Sharon felt a wave of slightly
hysterical laughter bubble up inside her.

Did Mike think that they needed some privacy? What
for? To indulge in the kind of conversation that couples
enjoyed? The only thing Matt could possibly want to tell
her was how much he disapproved of her discussing him
with a third party!

She swung round so that she could look him straight in
the eye. 'I assume you overheard the conversation just
now? At least you know that if there are any rumours flying
around they haven't come from me.'

'I haven't heard any rumours,' he said shortly. 'Nor
would I have expected them to come from you even if I
had.'

'Oh, wow! That sounded like a vote of confidence to me.
I must make a note of it. On August the twentieth Matthew
Dempster told me that I wasn't in any way to blame. A
genuine red-letter day!'

He swore softly. 'Stop it, Sharon! That won't achieve
anything and you know it.'

'Of course I do! I know that no matter what I do or say
it won't make any difference. Once you've made up your
mind then that's it, the decision is set in stone.'

She took a deep breath, realising that she was in danger
of saying something she would regret. 'Anyway, you'll be

pleased to know that the situation is about to change for the better.'

'Meaning what precisely?' he demanded in a tone that made a shiver run through her. She glanced at him uncertainly, not sure whether it was anger she could see in the depths of his eyes or some other equally powerful emotion.

She sighed when it hit her that even now she was making the mistake of looking for something that wasn't there. Matt would never love her so what was the point of torturing herself like that?

'Meaning that I have applied for another job. I decided that it would be better for everyone if I left here. And after what Mike has just said, about people noticing an atmosphere whenever you and I meet up, obviously it was the right decision.'

She shrugged, wishing he would say something instead of standing there watching her like that. 'I've an interview with my old team in London next week. Frankly, it's a formality. I know that I shall be offered the job.'

'I see. And you're sure this is what you want, Sharon?'

His tone was level to a fault. If he was pleased or saddened by the news, he gave no sign of either. Sharon fixed a smile to her mouth, wondering how it was possible to keep functioning when it felt as though she were slowly being ripped apart.

'I think it's the right thing to do. If I go back to London then I'll have all my old friends around me. It will make it easier to build a new life for myself.'

An expression of anguish crossed his face so quickly that she wasn't sure if she had actually seen it. 'Then I hope it works out well for you, Sharon. You deserve to be happy.'

It was obvious that he meant it. Sharon looked away when she felt her eyes fill with tears. 'Thank you. I…I'll hand in my notice as soon as I've been formally offered the job. But if you want to start advertising for someone to replace me, go ahead. If the London job does happen to fall through, I'm sure there will be others.'

'I'm sure there will be for someone with your experience,' he said flatly.

She shot him a wary look, unsure what she could hear in his voice at that moment. However, before she was able it work it out the alarm sounded. Matt took a deep breath and made an obvious effort to collect himself.

'Sounds like the first call of the day.' He went to the door and opened it for her. Sharon murmured her thanks as she passed him. Bert was already in the corridor, taking the message from Mike, and he looked round when she appeared.

'Injured fell walker in the Hambleton Hills. Broken leg and query possible other injuries,' he informed her.

'Right.' Sharon started along the corridor then paused when Matt laid a detaining hand on her arm.

'Take care, Sharon.'

She summoned a smile. 'I always do.'

'Maybe not all the time.' He gave her arm a quick squeeze then went into his office.

Sharon took a deep breath and hurried along the corridor, not allowing herself to wonder what he had meant. She couldn't deal with that as well as everything else. She quickly boarded the helicopter and fastened her seat belt. The ground whizzed past beneath them but she was cocooned in her own little world, a world where Matt had told her to take care because he cared what happened to her. How she wished she could stay in that world for ever!

The walker, a woman, was in a pretty bad state when they reached her. Her name was Debbie Wilson and she was with a party of fell walkers from a college in York. Fortunately, one of the group had had the good sense to lay out a marker of brightly coloured waterproofs so that they'd had no difficulty finding them. It was a very bleak part of the country, miles away from the nearest road, and Sharon could understand why they had been summoned to assist.

'Looks like a Pott's fracture to me,' she observed softly, studying the woman's left leg. The ankle was obviously dislocated and she was certain that both the tibia and fibula were broken as well.

'It really hurts,' Debbie whispered. 'And so does my face.'

She winced as she touched her left cheek. Sharon gently wiped away the blood that was trickling from the woman's nose as a result of the facial injury. 'It looks as though you've fractured your cheekbone, I'm afraid. There might be problems with your upper jaw as well, but the doctors will get you sorted out at the hospital so try not to worry.'

She glanced at Bert. 'Analgesics?'

'Yes. No point you being in pain when I've something in my box of tricks to help, is there, love?' he cheerfully told Debbie as he opened the case.

'D-don't want…injection! N-no…needles.' The young woman stuttered. Tears began to stream down her face, mingling with the blood that was coming from her nose, and she started to cough violently.

Sharon put a comforting arm around her. 'It's OK. If you don't want an injection then we won't force you to have one, Debbie. I promise.'

She frowned when she heard Debbie gasping for breath. The combination of the blood and tears, not to mention the swelling to her face, were restricting her breathing. It was a situation that could spiral out of control all too easily. Sharon knew that she had to calm the patient down as fast as she could.

'Now, you mustn't get upset. Nobody is going to do anything without your consent. If you don't want any painkillers then that's fine. We shall just get you on board the helicopter and take you straight to hospital.'

'C-can't go in that…!' Debbie shot a terrified look at the helicopter.

A young man suddenly stepped forward and crouched down beside them. 'Debs is terrified of flying,' he explained worriedly. 'She's tried everything to overcome her fear but nothing has worked.'

Sharon was at a loss to know what to do. She couldn't help wishing that someone had told them this sooner. Bert was obviously of the same opinion because he sighed as he stood up.

'I'll get Andy to contact base and see what they suggest, although it's going to be difficult getting an ambulance out here. We're miles away from the nearest road.'

He came back a few minutes later and drew Sharon aside. 'Ambulance control reckons it will take an hour and half to get a vehicle here. That's to the nearest road, mind, not actually to where we're standing.'

'Which means that Debbie will need to be carried to the road by stretcher.' She shook her head. 'Apart from the time that would take, it would be a nightmare for her to be carried over this terrain when she won't accept any pain relief. Then there's the fact that we have no idea what other injuries she has suffered. We *have* to convince her that she'll be better off travelling by helicopter.'

She went back to Debbie, frowning when she saw how ill the girl looked. She would bet a pound to a penny that Debbie had suffered some sort of internal injuries as well, making it imperative that they get her to hospital as quickly as possible.

'Debbie, we've been in touch with the ambulance control centre and it would take too long to get an ambulance here by road. I know you're scared of flying but you're going to have to be very, very brave.'

She squeezed the girl's hand. 'I don't want to frighten you but we must get you to hospital as fast as we can in case you have other injuries that we can't see.'

Debbie gulped. It was obvious that she was scared out of her wits. 'D-don't think I c-can...'

'Come on, Debs, you can do it!' The young man reached for her other hand and gripped it tightly. 'It's not like you to give up at the first hurdle, love!'

Debbie turned to him pleadingly. 'Will you come with me, Steve?'

'I don't know if I can.' He glanced at Sharon uncertainly and she immediately nodded. She knew that it was against the rules to let members of the public accompany a patient in the helicopter, but there simply wasn't any choice in this instance to her mind.

Bert looked concerned as they set about getting Debbie ready. 'Do you think we should have cleared this with base first?'

'Probably. But it would have taken even more time, wouldn't it?' She glanced at Debbie and shook her head. 'We can't afford to hang around here. We need to get her to hospital as fast as we can.'

'I suppose you're right,' Bert conceded.

They quickly loaded Debbie on board then got Steve settled and showed him how to strap himself in. He held Debbie's hand as Andy started the engines, squeezing it tightly as they took off.

Debbie gave a shrill cry of alarm. 'No! No! Let me out...!'

Sharon made a grab for her other arm when she started flailing it around. Fortunately, Debbie was strapped tightly to the stretcher but she was afraid that the girl would dislodge the intravenous drip. It was just unfortunate that Debbie somehow managed to catch Sharon a glancing blow across her face, knocking her backwards so that she hit her head on the bodywork of the helicopter. Even though she was wearing her helmet, the impact was still hard enough to make her see stars.

Sharon sank back into her seat and put her head between her knees while she tried to stave off the feeling of faintness. Debbie had stopped struggling now and was obviously shocked by what she had done.

'Are you OK?' Bert demanded in concern, putting his arm around her shoulders.

'I think so.' She took a wobbly breath but her head was still whirling and she felt sick. 'She's got a superb left hook!'

Everyone laughed at that. Whether it was the shock of what she had done or sheer fright, Debbie made no more fuss on the flight to the nearest hospital. Sharon didn't say anything to the others but she was glad when they reached their destination and she was able to get out of the helicopter. It had been sheer will-power that had kept her going during the last lap of the journey because she had felt so sick. It was a relief when she was able to climb out onto the tarmac.

She saw the hospital staff waiting to meet them and took a couple of steps towards them, then had the funniest feeling that the ground was rushing up to meet her. The next moment, she crumpled into an inglorious heap at their feet.

Sharon wasn't unconscious for long. By the time the staff had got her inside the building she had come round and was feeling rather foolish about having fainted. However, the A and E doctor on duty was adamant that she had to stay and be checked over despite her protests that she was fine.

She gave in with ill grace, feeling like a complete idiot when Bert came to tell her that they were going back to base. He was apologetic but she understood that they couldn't afford to have the air ambulance out of service while they waited with her.

An hour later Sharon was still waiting to be seen and chafing at the waste of time. She had just decided that she would sign herself out if nobody came to see her in the next five minutes when the cubicle curtain was swished aside. The words shrivelled up and died on her lips when Matt appeared rather than the young A and E doctor she had been expecting. She had no idea what he was doing there but the expression on his face told her that he wasn't pleased.

'What the hell did you think you were doing, you crazy woman? If the patient was too scared to travel by helicopter then you should have arranged for an ambulance to fetch her! It was a complete breach of protocol to have put yourself and everyone else at risk like that.'

Sharon summoned a smile because it seemed preferable to howling her eyes out. 'It's good to see you too, Matt. Come in. Don't worry if you haven't brought me any grapes. I didn't expect them.'

'Then you won't be disappointed, will you?'

He strode to the bed. Before she had time to realise what was happening he took hold of her and kissed her, then kissed her a second time and a third...

After that she simply stopped counting.

CHAPTER ELEVEN

How long the delicious interlude might have lasted wasn't clear, but Matt reluctantly let her go when the sound of footsteps announced that they were about to have company. Sharon barely had time to draw breath before the doctor appeared.

Matt quietly excused himself and left while Sharon was examined. Frankly, she was glad that the tests the young doctor made her do were so simple because she doubted whether she could have coped with anything more complicated! Had Matt really been here and kissed her as though…as though his very life depended on it?

She obediently answered the doctor's questions and followed his finger as he moved it about in front of her eyes, then she was free to go. She left the cubicle, hardly daring to breathe in case Matt had been a figment of her imagination. However, he was sitting in the waiting area and he got up the moment she appeared.

'Are you OK?' he asked, his voice grating with an emotion that made her feel dizzy all over again.

'Fine,' she whispered in a tone that wouldn't have convinced anyone she was telling the truth. She took a deep breath and looked straight at him. 'What's going on, Matt? Why did you do what you just did?'

'How very delicately you phrase things, Miss Lennard.' His green eyes glinted with amusement and a host of other things that sent her poor head into yet another spin.

He laughed when he saw her bemused expression. Placing an arm around her shoulders, he gently guided her towards the exit. 'I did it because I couldn't help myself. I've been fighting this for far too long, Sharon. I have finally admitted defeat.'

He didn't say anything more, leaving her seething with questions as they made their way to his car. Once they were there, he stopped and turned her to face him, and the expression on his face was everything she could have wished for.

'I'm mad about you, Sharon. I knew you were going to cause me trouble the moment I set eyes on you at your interview, and I was right.' He tilted her face so that he could kiss her then sighed. 'I know how badly I've behaved but I'm hoping that you'll forgive me.'

'I might.' She saw him frown and laughed shakily because his next answer was so important to her. 'Would you mind explaining exactly what being *mad* about me means?'

'Typical woman! Chooses the worst moment possible to be pedantic.' His smile showed her that he was teasing her while the tone of his voice told her all sorts of other things.

Sharon shivered when she heard the underlying message it held. The trouble was that she was afraid to let herself believe what he seemed to be saying until he had confirmed it in words of one syllable so that there could be no mistake.

'I'm sorry but I still need you to explain,' she told him quietly.

'I love you, Sharon. That's what I meant. Does that explanation meet with your approval?' he said gently.

Oh, it did! It most certainly did!

She flung her arms around his neck and kissed him, feeling her heart overflowing with happiness. The kiss was both a seal and a promise and would have lasted far longer than it did if they hadn't been interrupted yet again.

'I hate to butt in where I'm obviously not wanted, but I sense a story here.'

They both turned and stared bemusedly at the young man who had accosted them. He held out his hand and grinned at them. 'Geoff Goodison from the *Weekly News*. We met when you were airlifting that prem baby, if you remember.'

Sharon dazedly shook his hand. 'Oh. Yes.'

'I'm here following up a story and just happened to spot you two,' he explained. 'While I hate to intrude I've got a feeling that there's another wonderful human interest story here.'

He looked pointedly at them and Sharon blushed. Matt, however, seemed quite unperturbed. Looping his arm around Sharon's shoulders, he looked steadily at the other man.

'You could be right but I don't want to go jumping the gun, if you catch my drift. Do me a favour and get lost, will you?'

Geoff laughed good-naturedly. 'Will do, but only on condition I get an exclusive!' He handed Matt his card. 'Give me a call once everything has been sorted out. Oh, and the best of luck!'

Matt sighed ruefully as he tucked the card into his pocket. 'I've a feeling that I'm going to need more than a *bit* of luck. How many *more* interruptions are we going to get?'

'Maybe this isn't the best place in the world to talk,' she suggested with a chuckle.

'I wasn't thinking of doing much talking!' he growled, kissing her swiftly. He unlocked the car and helped her into the passenger seat. 'Let's go someplace quiet before I go completely crazy!'

Sharon laughed as he slid behind the wheel. 'I thought we had already established that you weren't mad?'

'We have. And I'm not.' He kissed her again. 'But frustration can do untold damage to a man and that's a well-documented fact.'

'We certainly can't run the risk of that happening.' She gave a sudden groan. 'But I'm needed back at base. I can't just go taking the rest of the day off when there's nothing wrong with me.'

'I'm not having you flying again today,' Matt said sternly. 'I've already arranged cover so you're to go home and take things easy.'

'But I'm fine, Matt,' she protested. 'Honestly, I am.'

She got no further because he stopped her in the most effective way possible. Sharon's eyes drifted shut as she returned his kiss, wondering bemusedly if the stars she was seeing this time were real. She could barely think straight when Matt let her go and he took immediate advantage of her weakened state.

'No more arguments now. It would be foolish to fly again today after that bang you had on your head. Doctor's orders—understand?'

She nodded dreamily, settling back in the seat while he started the engine. 'Has anybody told you how bossy you are, Matthew Dempster?'

'Frequently!' He grinned at her. 'It's one of my better faults. Think you can put up with it?'

'I might be persuaded to,' she said, smiling wickedly at him.

He gave a heartfelt groan. 'Don't do that! Not if you want us to get home in one piece.' He lifted her hand to his lips and pressed a kiss to her palm. 'Have you any idea what you do to me, Miss Lennard?'

'Not really, but I'm willing to let you show me.'

He smiled at her and there was such love in his eyes that she felt her heart swell with joy. 'A woman after my own heart, it appears.'

She smiled back at him. 'I only ever wanted your heart, Matt. That plus the chance to be a part of your life.'

'You will be…you *are*. I can't imagine my life without you, Sharon. I don't want to try.' He shuddered expressively and she quickly leant over and kissed him on the cheek.

'You don't have to try. We're going to spend the rest of our lives together, Matt. You, me and—'

'Jessica,' he finished for her. 'I love you, Sharon.'

'And I love you, Matt,' she whispered, smiling at him with her heart in her eyes.

'That's all I needed to hear!'

They drove straight to Sharon's house. Matt parked outside then followed her up the path. Sharon unlocked the door, thinking how different everywhere looked to how it had done that morning. The sun seemed to be warmer, the scent of the flowers seemed even sweeter. The fact that Matt loved her made everything seem so much better than it had a few short hours before.

He took her into his arms as soon as she had closed the front door, holding her close as he kissed her over and over again as though he couldn't get enough of the taste of her. Sharon gave herself up to his kisses, glorying in the fact that he wanted her so much. It seemed the most natural thing in the world when he swung her up into his arms, carried her into her bedroom and laid her gently on the bed.

'I love you, Sharon,' he whispered as his hands moved to the hem of her T-shirt and drew it up over her head. He undid the snap on her jeans and slid them down her hips then tossed them onto the floor.

She smiled back at him, loving the way his eyes had darkened as he turned to look at her. All she had on now were sensible cotton briefs and a matching bra, the type of underwear which she normally wore for work. However, it seemed to make little difference to Matt that the undergarments weren't adorned with oodles of lace.

'I love you too,' she replied softly, reaching up to unbutton his shirt. The tiny pearl buttons proved oddly recalcitrant, unless it was the fact that her hands were trembling that was causing her so much trouble.

Sharon frowned as she struggled to work them free, looking up in surprise when Matt laughed softly. 'You need some practice from the look of it,' he teased, bending to brush a kiss over her parted lips.

Sharon shivered when she felt the gentle thrust of his tongue seeking entry into her mouth. Her hands stopped struggling with the buttons and fastened instead on a fold of his shirt while she drew him to her. They fell back against the pillows and she gasped when she felt his weight settling over her, felt the urgent thrusting of his body against hers.

Matt groaned deeply as he reared back and ripped the shirt over his head then quickly dispensed with the rest of his clothing. 'I didn't realise it was possible to want anyone this much! I love you, Sharon.'

The words were swallowed up as he kissed her. Sharon felt them being absorbed into her body, filling her heart and soul with an overwhelming sense of joy. She closed her eyes and opened her heart to him. If she'd had any lingering doubts about her role in his life they had disappeared. Matt needed her, now and for evermore!

Night was drawing in when Sharon slipped out of bed. Matt was still asleep, his head pillowed on his arm, his body lying relaxed and at ease. She paused to drop a kiss on the back of his neck, smiling when he murmured her name. It was good to know that, asleep or awake, she had found a very special place in his heart.

Pulling on a robe, she went first to the bathroom and showered then made her way to the kitchen. They hadn't had anything to eat since they'd come home and she was starving, and knew that Matt would be, too, when he woke up.

It took no time at all to whiz up an omelette and toss a salad. She added a pot of coffee to the tray then carried everything back to the bedroom for an impromptu picnic. Matt had just woken up and he smiled sleepily at her.

'How did you know I was starving?'

'Because I was.' She set the tray on the chest of drawers then leant over to kiss him, laughing when he immediately pulled her into his arms and rolled her over so that he could make the most of the opportunity. The kiss was long and deliciously thorough, and Matt sighed regretfully when it came to an end.

'I would dearly love to continue this, but I'm so hungry I'm afraid my strength might give out. I'd hate to disappoint you.'

'You'd never do that,' she told him, quickly scooting out of reach when he made a grab for her. 'Now be good. It would be a shame to waste all this lovely food.'

'Yes, ma'am!' He gave her a mocking salute then took the plate she offered him and hungrily attacked the omelette. 'This is good. My compliments to the chef.'

'Thank you kindly, sir.' She picked up her own plate then laughed. 'I must say that this is the first time I've ever had dinner in bed!'

'It's a first for me, too.' His eyes were awash with tenderness as he smiled at her. 'But everything we do together feels as though it's the first time it's ever happened, sweetheart.'

'Thank you,' she whispered, her eyes misting because she knew what he was telling her.

'You don't have to thank me for telling the truth.' He put down his plate then took hers from her so that he could pull her into his arms. 'What we have is unique, the result of how we feel about each other.'

He took a deep breath but there was no hesitation before he continued. 'Claire and I had a good marriage but I never felt the same way about her as I feel about you. That was one of the reasons I was so determined to keep you at arm's length.'

'What do you mean?' she queried, shocked by the revelation.

'That I felt guilty. I loved Claire but it was a gentle kind of love, the sort of love you feel for a friend, I suppose. When I realised how deep my feelings were for you, it seemed wrong. Claire was dead and here I was, falling madly in love with another woman in a way I could never have loved her. It seemed like…like a betrayal of her and everything we'd had together.'

Sharon heard the pain in his voice and her heart ached for him. She put her arms around him, willing him to see that he mustn't punish himself for feeling this way. 'It isn't a betrayal of her! It doesn't take away anything from your relationship with Claire just because you've fallen in love with me. You must see that, Matt.'

'I do—now.' He kissed her swiftly then determinedly put her away from him again. Sharon sensed that he needed to talk through his feelings and knew how important it was. Before Matt could move forward, he had to be able to put the past behind him with a clear heart.

'I realised that I can't live in the past any longer, and that Claire wouldn't have wanted me to. Guilt isn't a good basis to build your life on, is it?'

'Does that mean you've accepted that you weren't responsible for the accident as well? That was all part and parcel of your reluctance to let me into your life, wasn't it?' she queried softly.

'I think I shall always feel a little bit to blame even though I know it's foolish,' he admitted. 'I can't help it because every time I look at Jessica I'm reminded of how differently her life might have turned out. The difference is that I'm no longer emotionally crippled by constantly blaming myself. It was an accident and I've accepted that.'

'Oh, I'm so glad, Matt!' Sharon couldn't hold back her tears because she had feared that this moment might never come. She heard him sigh as he pulled her into his arms again and laughed shakily. 'Sorry, I'm making you all wet!'

'I don't care. I just hate to see you getting upset like this,' he declared thickly.

'I'm not crying because I'm unhappy! Just the opposite, in fact.' She brushed a tender kiss over his mouth, let her lips find the adorable dimple in his chin then gave them permission to linger...

Matt shuddered. 'Keep that up and we'll never get to the coffee stage!' he said thickly.

She chuckled, knowing that he was teasing her because he couldn't bear to see her upset. 'Thinking about your stomach already, Dr Dempster? I thought that only happened when a couple had nothing better to think about.'

'That is never going to happen with us!' He rolled her over and kissed her then let his mouth glide down her throat until it reached the hardened peak of her breast. Sharon moaned as a wave of longing enveloped her once more but he was completely ruthless as he sat up again. 'Mmm, I think I might just have convinced you?'

'Sadist!' she said, accusingly, glaring at him because her whole body was throbbing in the most uncomfortable fashion.

'Is that a nice thing to say to the man you're going to marry?' he demanded.

'Marry? I can't recall that subject being mentioned before. I believe it's customary for the prospective bridegroom to ask the woman he wants to marry if she will do him the honour, rather than take her agreement for granted,' she shot back, doling out a dose of his own medicine even though her pulse was racing at the thought of marrying him.

It was hard to believe what was happening when a few hours ago she had been making plans never to see him again.

'Is that so? Tut-tut, I really should have checked up on the right procedure before I jumped in. Still, I suppose it can wait till later.'

Matt smiled wickedly when he heard her gasp. It was obvious that he was playing her at her own game as he settled her comfortably in his arms again. 'Now, where was I before I got sidetracked? Ah, yes. Jessica.' He suddenly sighed. 'She's another reason I was determined not to get involved with you.'

'Because you didn't want her getting hurt? You already explained that to me, Matt, and I understand,' Sharon said quickly, putting aside her disappointment at the way he had brushed aside the subject of them getting married.

'It wasn't only that, Sharon. Obviously, I wanted to protect Jessica but I also wanted to protect you. Looking after a disabled child isn't easy. There are all sorts of problems to contend with, from the physical to the practical. It didn't seem fair to burden you with them, not after you had given up a whole year of your life to care for your father. I felt it would be taking advantage of you.'

'Oh, Matt, you are an idiot! Don't you know how much I love Jessica?' She turned to face him, needing to convince him that she was telling the truth. 'I know it won't be easy. I have no illusions that it will be. But I want to help you take care of her. I'd feel privileged, in fact, if you would let me.'

His eyes darkened as he cupped her cheek. 'I don't know why I've been so lucky as to find you, sweetheart. Someone, somewhere, must be on my side—that's all I can think. But you are sure that you understand what you would be taking on? Jessica isn't going to regain her mobility unless a miracle happens. Obviously, I shall do everything in my power to make sure that she can live an independent life, but—'

'No buts! I understand. I know there could be problems and that there are bound to be pressures at times…' She stopped and stared at him. 'That's why you didn't ask me to visit her in hospital, isn't it? Because you felt that it would be taking advantage of me?'

'Yes.' He sighed. 'When I got home that day and discovered that Jessica was ill, it hit me like a bolt out of the blue. I realised that, no matter how I felt about you, it wouldn't be fair to involve you any further. Why should you spend your life worrying about my daughter?'

'Because I want to.' She kissed him slowly then smiled into his eyes. 'But most of all because I love you, Matt, and want to share all the bad times in your life as well as the good ones. It's all part and parcel of loving someone.'

'Oh, darling!'

He drew her to him and held her close, held her as though he had no intention of ever letting her go. Sharon sincerely hoped that was so because she had no intention of letting him live the rest of his life without her!

'To think that I came so close to losing you,' he muttered, his voice breaking with emotion.

'I never wanted to leave,' she admitted. 'I just couldn't handle the thought of being around you and not being part of your life. That's the only reason I decided to apply for another job.'

He drew back and looked at her. 'I'm glad that you did.' He must have seen her surprise because he smiled tenderly at her. 'It came as such a shock when you told me this morning that you would be leaving. It forced me to take a long, hard look at the situation. I think I had started to realise what a mistake I was making by driving you away when Bert radioed in and told me that you were in hospital. I was terrified that I was going to lose you.'

Sharon frowned. 'Didn't Bert explain that I'd just had a knock on the head?'

'No, he didn't. To be honest, he scared the wits out of me, told me that nobody knew how seriously injured you were.' Matt suddenly laughed. 'Ever had a feeling that we've been set up?'

'You mean that Bert *deliberately* let you think that I was at death's door?' she exclaimed. 'Oh, I'm sure he wouldn't have done such a thing…would he?'

'Let's just say that I have my suspicions.' Matt grinned at her. 'If it was a set-up to get us together then it worked. So now all we need to do is decide when we're going to get married and *everyone* will be happy.'

'Aren't you forgetting something?' she queried, her brows arching. 'There's still the little matter of a proposal first.'

'Oh, *that*! Well, I suppose if you insist…'

He suddenly leapt out of the bed and went down on one knee. 'I love you, Sharon Lennard, so will you do me the honour of becoming my wife?'

He should have looked ridiculous, kneeling there naked whilst uttering the formal words, but he didn't. Sharon only had to see the tender light of adoration in his eyes to know how much this moment meant to Matt as well as to her.

She held out her hand and smiled at him with her heart in her eyes. 'Yes, Matt. I'll marry you. I love you so—'

She didn't get a chance to finish the sentence as Matt swept her into his arms.

EPILOGUE

'HAVE you seen this?'

Sharon looked up as Matt came back with the post. She shaded her eyes against the glare of the October sun, feeling too lazy to actually sit up and look at what he was showing her.

It was the second week of their honeymoon, which they were spending at his parents' villa in Spain. Mr and Mrs Dempster had offered to let them use it and had insisted on looking after Jessica while they were away. So far it had been everything she could have wished for—long, lazy days spent by the pool, wonderful nights spent in each other's arms. The perfect honeymoon to follow on from a wonderful wedding day.

The ceremony had taken place in the local parish church and she would never forget the look on Matt's face as he had watched her walking down the aisle on his father's arm. Jessica had been her bridesmaid and she had looked as pretty as a picture in a white dress, patterned all over with tiny pink rosebuds, which had matched the ones that had adorned her wheelchair. There had been scarcely a dry eye in the church as the congregation had watched her following Sharon down the aisle.

After that had come the reception. Bert, in his role as best man, had read out the cards and messages, including one from the men on the oil rig. Sharon had ruefully shaken her head when Bert had repeated their invitation to her and Matt to spend their honeymoon there! Spain had seemed a far more attractive option, and she hadn't been disappointed...

'I don't know what that smug smile is for but I shall make it my business to find out later, you understand?'

She laughed when she realised that Matt was still waiting for her to say something. 'Promises, promises! Anyway, what have you got there?'

'Mum has sent us a copy of the local weekly paper.' He sat down on the end of the sun lounger and grinned at her. 'Guess who's in it?'

Sharon gasped as he held up the paper so that she could see the photograph taking up much of the front page. It was a picture of them leaving the church after their wedding. She vaguely remembered spotting the journalist on the fringes of the crowd, but hadn't taken much notice.

'Did you know that journalist was going to do a feature for the paper?' she demanded.

'I had an idea, shall we say.' Matt smiled as he looked at the paper again. 'It's all good publicity now that the trust has launched an appeal to fund another helicopter. The area health authority has promised to match every pound we raise so, hopefully, this will prompt people to dig deeper into their pockets.'

'I never realised how mercenary you could be, Matthew Dempster! I'm surprised you didn't offer to sell our wedding pictures to one of those gossip magazines.'

'Now, why didn't *I* think of that!' He laughed when she gasped in outrage. 'I'm only teasing. By the way, did I tell you that Jessica is having a bring-and-buy sale while we're away? She wants to do her bit to help raise money for the new helicopter.'

'Oh, how sweet! Isn't she a great kid, Matt?'

'She is. And she feels the same way about you. I have never seen her looking so happy as she did on our wedding day, even though I don't think it came as a surprise to her when we announced that we were getting married.'

'Why do you say that?' Sharon frowned.

'Because I got the distinct impression that my mother had been putting ideas into her head, not that she really needed encouraging, mind you. Jessica loved you from the outset but, then, she does take after her father in so many ways.'

'Is that a fact?' she asked, laughing at him.

'It is. An indisputable one, too. But that's quite enough time wasted on talking. I can think of better things to do at this moment.'

He scooped her up in his arms. Sharon wrapped her arms around his neck as he carried her back inside the villa. She shot a last look at the paper lying abandoned beside the pool and smiled when she read the caption above the photograph.

Love was most *definitely* in the air!

MILLS & BOON®

Makes any time special™

Mills & Boon publish 29 new titles every month. Select from...

Modern Romance™   Tender Romance™

Sensual Romance™

Medical Romance™   Historical Romance™

MAT2

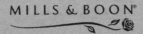

MILLS & BOON®

Medical Romance™

EMOTIONAL RESCUE by *Alison Roberts*

Newly qualified ambulance officer Hannah Duncan soon realises that she loves her job – and her colleague Adam Lewis! But he doesn't want children, and Hannah already has a toddler of her own. Will she be able to help rescue Adam from the demons of his past and give them all a future?

THE SURGEON'S DILEMMA by *Laura MacDonald*

Catherine Slade knew she was deeply attracted to her boss, the charismatic senior consultant Paul Grantham. She also knew he had a secret sorrow that she could help him with. If only a relationship between them wasn't so forbidden…

A FULL RECOVERY by *Gill Sanderson*

Book two of Nursing Sisters duo

If he is to persuade emotionally bruised theatre nurse Jo to love again, neurologist Ben Franklin must give her tenderness and patience. But when she does eventually give herself to him, how can he be sure she's not just on the rebound?

On sale 3rd August 2001

Available at most branches of WH Smith, Tesco, Martins, Borders, Easons, Sainsbury, Woolworth and most good paperback bookshops 0701/03a

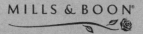

MILLS & BOON®

Medical Romance™

EMERGENCY REUNION *by Abigail Gordon*

The man she had loved and lost eight years before was back in Dr Hannah Morgan's life as her new boss! Now a father, Kyle Templeton was still bitter, but Hannah was beginning to wonder if all three of them had been given a second chance.

A BABY FOR JOSEY *by Rebecca Lang*

When Nurse Josey Lincoln confided in Dr Guy Lake about her desperate fear that she could never have a baby – he offered to help! But even if he could give her a baby, he couldn't give her *himself*, and she began to realise that she wanted Guy most of all…

THE VISITING CONSULTANT *by Leah Martyn*

When Josh meets nurse Alex Macleay during a medical emergency, the mutual attraction is too much to ignore. He wants a casual summer affair, but Alex wants a husband and a father for her little girl – and Josh is the ideal candidate!

On sale 3rd August 2001

Available at most branches of WH Smith, Tesco, Martins, Borders, Easons, Sainsbury, Woolworth and most good paperback bookshops

0701/03b

A
Perfect Family

An enthralling family saga by bestselling author

PENNY
JORDAN

Published 20th July

*Available at branches of WH Smith, Tesco,
Martins, RS McCall, Forbuoys, Borders, Easons,
Sainsbury, Woolworth and most good paperback bookshops*

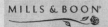

4 FREE

books and a surprise gift!

We would like to take this opportunity to thank you for reading this Mills & Boon® book by offering you the chance to take FOUR more specially selected titles from the Medical Romance™ series absolutely FREE! We're also making this offer to introduce you to the benefits of the Reader Service™—

- ★ FREE home delivery
- ★ FREE gifts and competitions
- ★ FREE monthly Newsletter
- ★ Exclusive Reader Service discounts
- ★ Books available before they're in the shops

Accepting these FREE books and gift places you under no obligation to buy, you may cancel at any time, even after receiving your free shipment. Simply complete your details below and return the entire page to the address below. *You don't even need a stamp!*

YES! Please send me 4 free Medical Romance books and a surprise gift. I understand that unless you hear from me, I will receive 6 superb new titles every month for just £2.49 each, postage and packing free. I am under no obligation to purchase any books and may cancel my subscription at any time. The free books and gift will be mine to keep in any case.

M1ZEA

Ms/Mrs/Miss/Mr ....Initials...................................
BLOCK CAPITALS PLEASE

Surname ....

Address ....

....

....Postcode...................................

Send this whole page to:
UK: FREEPOST CN81, Croydon, CR9 3WZ
EIRE: PO Box 4546, Kilcock, County Kildare (stamp required)

Offer valid in UK and Eire only and not available to current Reader Service subscribers to this series. We reserve the right to refuse an application and applicants must be aged 18 years or over. Only one application per household. Terms and prices subject to change without notice. Offer expires 31st January 2002. As a result of this application, you may receive offers from other carefully selected companies. If you would prefer not to share in this opportunity please write to The Data Manager at the address above.

Mills & Boon® is a registered trademark owned by Harlequin Mills & Boon Limited.
Medical Romance™ is being used as a trademark.